MY HEART TO HOLD

A MAXWELL FAMILY SAGA - BOOK TWO

S.B. ALEXANDER

RAVEN WING PUBLISHING

My Heart to Hold
A Maxwell Family Saga - Book Two
Copyright © 2019 by S.B. Alexander
All rights reserved.
First Edition:
E-book ISBN-13: 978-1-7329767-2-6
Print ISBN-13: 978-1-7329767-3-3

Visit: http://sbalexander.com
Editor: Red Adept Editing
Cover Design by Hang Le

This is a work of fiction. Names, characters, places and incidents either are the product of the author's imagination or are used fictitiously, and any resemblance to locales, events, business establishments, or actual persons-living or dead-is entirely coincidental.

Chapter 1

Quinn

Excitement comingled with dread as I walked down the hall toward my locker. My stomach was in knots, my hands were sweaty, and my mind worked overtime as I scanned the scarcely filled halls, looking more for Maiken than Tessa.

I didn't know how Tessa was going to act when she saw me. I hadn't seen Tessa since two weeks ago when she had not-so-accidentally pushed me into the pool. I would bet she would be her same old harridan self. Then again, maybe the freezing temps of the pool water had knocked some sense into her. Maybe she would be a new Tessa—nicer, friendlier.

I couldn't say I was a different Quinn, at least not yet. I had no idea how I would handle Tessa if she lashed out at me. I was so nervous, I'd chewed my nails all the way to school. But I was also dying to see Maiken, and at the moment, that trumped any dread I felt over what Tessa had up her sleeve for me.

Maiken and his family had gone to Georgia for Christmas. His mom had decided at the last minute to visit her sister. We'd exchanged several texts, but that had been it. Nevertheless, the two weeks without Maiken had been lonely and depressing. I almost felt like I'd dreamt I had a boyfriend.

My heart pitter-pattered with each step I took toward my locker. A handful of students lingered, gushing about what they'd gotten for Christmas or what they'd done over the break. My two weeks had been filled with family stuff and chores, as usual. As far as presents, I'd gotten mostly money and a new saddle for Apple that I'd been wanting.

My best friend, Celia, had gone skiing with her family up in Vermont. She'd asked me to join her, but I didn't know how to ski and didn't care to learn. Instead, I found myself skating on the Maxwell lake along with Kade's wife, Lacey, who had wanted to try her hand at the sport. Momma didn't want me to be on the lake alone. When I'd asked Eleanor Maxwell if she would be around, she'd informed me that she and Martin were leaving on a month-long vacation.

"I'm sorry, Quinn," Eleanor had said. "Kade and Lacey will be watching the house until Maiken and his family return. Why don't you check with them? I'm sure Lacey might be up for skating."

I'd raised an eyebrow when she mentioned Lacey and skating. To my surprise, Lacey had always wanted to try the sport but never had the chance.

I pulled out my phone and sent Maiken a text. *Will you be at school today?* I tried calling him the day before, but he hadn't answered. I'd also sent him a text, but he hadn't responded. I chalked up the silence to him driving the family back to Ashford.

I stood at my locker, staring at my phone, waiting for the three little bouncing dots that indicated he was typing a reply to appear. After several seconds, no dots or any sign that Maiken had read my text.

More voices peppered the air as the hall began to fill with students.

"Quinn!" Celia bounced up to my locker. Her espresso-colored hair was twisted up on her head, her cheeks were stained pink, and her eyes were swimming with happiness. "Guess what?"

"Tessa is going to boarding school?" I was teasing… but deep down, I wasn't.

Her sculpted eyebrows lifted above her black-rimmed glasses. "Really?"

I giggled. "No, silly. What's up? You were finally brave enough to ski down a black diamond?" That was all she'd talked about before she left.

She wrinkled her button nose, which was red from the cold or maybe sunburned. "I chickened out. The wind was too brutal." She extracted a flyer from her purse. "I saw this on the announcement board outside the admin office. The school paper has an opening."

"That's great." I sounded down in the dumps when I should've been excited for my best friend. She'd wanted to work on the school's newspaper since freshman year.

"What's wrong? Are you worried about Tessa?"

I scanned the hall but still didn't see Maiken. And since we were on the topic of my enemy, I didn't see Tessa either. A cold chill zinged down my spine. Maybe Maiken had decided he didn't want to date me anymore. Or maybe his mom had decided to stay in Georgia. Maybe something bad had happened to him. Or maybe, and this one was out there, Tessa had gotten him to somehow, and he'd had a change of heart about our relationship. After all, she had bragged that I hadn't won anything yet when I'd stormed out of her house at her holiday party.

Stop freaking out. He probably got in late last night.

"I haven't heard from Maiken since Friday."

She swatted me lightly. "Don't think the worst. He'll be here." She sounded so sure.

I wished I had her confidence. *You better find some quickly if you're going to be a different Quinn.*

"Do you know something I don't?" I asked.

"The basketball team needs him."

I snorted. "He was suspended for three games. I doubt Coach is eager to have Chase and Maiken punching it out on the court again." I checked my phone once more.

She covered my screen with her hand. "Take a breath. If he doesn't show, then we'll go down to Georgia."

I feigned a smile, although I was all for the idea.

She opened her locker. "So if I get on the school newspaper, I want to cover sports."

I pressed my shoulder into the locker. "Really?" I shouldn't have been surprised. She was into skiing and loved going to football games and basketball games. She even enjoyed skating. "I thought you wanted to write about the issues we face at school?"

"Nah. That's boring and doesn't involve cute boys." She giggled.

I joined in, and the tension eased slightly.

"See? I got you to laugh. For real, though. Sports is my new thing." She closed her locker. "Okay, back to Tessa. If she dishes out any shit, stand up to her like you did at her party."

I gnawed on a hangnail, praying I could. I hadn't changed at all in two weeks. I was still Quinn Thompson. I still lived on a farm, stuttered when I was nervous, spit out random facts, and didn't like confrontation. Not only that, I wasn't a bully and wasn't about to resort to being one either. My brother's fights had done nothing but incite more violence, and that wasn't in my nature.

Glancing past me, Celia flicked her chin. "See? I told you he would return."

As if in slow motion, I swiveled my head, and my heartbeat ramped up from idle to a hundred beats per minute.

Maiken strutted down the hall. His skin was tanned, and his

long legs ate up the space as he remained absorbed with something on his phone.

I stared, willing him to look up—to look at me. Maybe he was texting me. But my phone, which was tethered to my hand, didn't vibrate or alert me to a text.

Girls ogled him, some tittering, others whispering, and I spied some blushing. I couldn't blame them. I felt like I was noticing him for the first time all over again. His sandy-blond hair was unruly on top as though the wind had whipped up its own hairstyle for Maiken. His black T-shirt stretched across his broad chest and hung over his tattered jeans, and he had a confident aura about him as if he owned the world.

I even ogled the boy who before long would also own my heart. Or maybe he already did and I was too scared to acknowledge it. Nevertheless, I couldn't believe a handsome boy like Maiken was into me. At times, I worried that I would wake up one day, and he would be gone.

"Go see him," Celia said.

I wanted to run and jump into his arms, but my feet and legs seemed glued to the shiny white floor. Honestly, I wanted him to look up and acknowledge me. I wanted that connection we had in which our gazes melded together from afar as though no one around us existed.

Then as if glass had shattered somewhere near me, my dreamy state turned into a nightmare as Tessa all but skipped down the hall, calling out to Maiken.

I gritted my teeth as anger set in.

She bounced up to Maiken, her black ponytail swinging in the wind. "Wait up."

Maiken came to a full stop in the middle of the hall, actually waiting for the harridan.

My heart fell to the floor.

Don't scream. Don't cry.

Her fingers went around his arm, guiding him out of traffic. Then her mouth started moving.

I couldn't hear what she was saying over the other voices in the hall. Or maybe the pounding of my pulse in my ears masked all other sound.

Maiken listened to Tessa intently as if she were telling him a riveting story.

What in the world?

Huffing, I stomped down the hall, pushing my way through students tall and short, big and small. A cloud of fury hung over me, and with each step I took, I swore that cloud would open up and rain down on Tessa if she didn't get her paws off of Maiken.

This was not how I envisioned my first day back at school or my first time seeing Maiken in two weeks. Then again, where Tessa was involved, all bets were off the table.

Momma had made a point to tell me that morning that fighting wasn't the answer in solving problems. But wars were won by fighting on the battlefield. At the moment, my battlefield was the school hallway, and my enemy was about to get what was coming to her.

Celia rushed up to me. "I got your back."

My hands were fisted at my sides, and my nails dug into my palms the closer I got.

"Watch this," a boy said to his friend as I passed them.

I'd never punched someone before. But I imagined bone hitting bone hurt.

"First day back, and we're already going to see trouble," the same boy said in an excited tone as though he lived for those moments.

The word *trouble* catapulted me out of my haze, and Momma's reprimand rang loud and clear in my head. "If I hear you're fighting or you get in trouble in school, you will not be allowed to date Maiken."

She knew how to hit a nerve. I certainly didn't want to mess up my chances of dating Maiken. Besides, somehow I had to put Tessa in her place. I couldn't let her continue to bully me. The problem was that I had no clue how to get her to back off.

Flaring my nostrils while looking at Tessa, I enclosed Maiken's hand in mine. "Hey, there you are."

He flinched for some reason, and a stabbing pain poked my chest. I shifted my eyes from Tessa to him, on the verge of tears. But when Maiken's slow grin emerged as his gaze roamed all over me, any doubts I had about him and me vanished.

Tessa sneered. "This is a private conversation."

Ignore her. You haven't seen your boyfriend in two weeks. Steal him away. Find a hiding spot and don't come out until high school is over. I smiled at the thought of blinking away my high school years mainly to avoid Tessa. But I was living in a fairytale, especially when Celia's acid tone burned through my senses.

"Private?" Celia got in Tessa's personal space. "Right? All you're trying to do is start trouble."

Tessa puffed out her chest. "Shut up, Celia."

I was tempted to let Celia and Tessa duke it out. But I couldn't let my best friend get sent to the principal's office on my behalf.

A crowd started to form around us.

Tessa swung her dark gaze to me. "And I thought you would be the one to start a fight." Her condescending tone scraped along my arms as though my cat, Betty, were dragging her claws over them.

"T-the day is y-young," I stuttered out. *Damn nervous habit.*

She pouted. "Aw, she still stutters."

I let go of Maiken and fisted my hands at my sides.

Remember, no trouble, or you won't be allowed to date Maiken.

Tessa let out a laugh that dared me to hit her. "You wouldn't."

"Babe," Maiken drawled. "She wants you to hit her."

The word babe rolled off his lips and melted the icy anger that had taken over my body.

The bell rang, and Tessa hiked her bag over her shoulder. "Still the same old scared Quinn, who can't stand up for herself." She shook her head. "Maiken, we'll talk after school." Then she ambled away, her head held high.

"What is sh-she talking about?" I asked Maiken, who was shaking his head.

If he were chumming up to Tessa, I would definitely punch her, despite my mom's edict.

"Some cheerleader basketball fundraiser."

Celia's lips parted. "Oh, that." She hooked her arm in mine. "Come on, Quinn. I'll tell you all about it. It's nothing to worry about."

Like heck. When it came to Tessa, I had to worry.

Maiken grasped my other arm. "She'll catch up with you, Celia."

The final bell hadn't rung yet, so we had time. Besides, my classroom was only two doors down.

"Don't be late for class." Celia faded from view.

The hall had all but emptied except for two students running by Maiken and me.

He drank me in from head to toe. "I'm sorry I didn't text you back. My phone died, and I didn't have my charger with me. I missed you." Sadness threaded through the last three words.

I was about to tell him I missed him too when his lips were on mine, kissing me like I was his world. In that moment, I was the luckiest girl ever to walk the halls of Kensington High.

Chapter 2

Maiken

I inhaled several times, walking in a circle as I tried to catch my breath. I hated running suicides, but we started every basketball practice with them.

A handful of girls and one guy sat in the bleachers, watching us practice and watching the cheerleaders going through their routine in one corner of the gym. I kept looking for Quinn. I hadn't seen her since I'd kissed the lights out of her that morning.

The two weeks away from her had been dreadful in some ways and great in others. I'd thought about her nonstop. I wished she'd been with me, hanging on the beach in Georgia where my aunt Denise lived. I wished she'd been there to hold my hand when I'd woken up on Christmas morning, feeling empty and sad that my dad wasn't with us. Yet on the flip side, it had been great to spend time with my brothers, sisters, Mom, and Aunt Denise.

I stopped and wiped the sweat off my face with my T-shirt as Liam came over doing the same. He regarded me with amber eyes that reminded me of his sister, Quinn. "I feel like I'm out of shape. So how was Georgia?"

It didn't matter how in shape I was—suicides were brutal. I lifted a shoulder. "Warm." That was the only answer I had. He didn't need to hear how I'd cried all day on Christmas or that the pain over my dad's death was as sharp and gut-wrenching as the day he'd died.

Four months had passed since we'd buried him, and that day when the two military men had knocked on our door to tell us he'd been killed on a battlefield in Iraq was as bright as the North Star was on a clear, crisp night. I knew my mom was feeling the same way because I'd heard her quiet cries in the middle of the night when I'd lain awake, staring at a ceiling fan turn and turn and turn.

Coach blew his whistle. "Split into two teams. Starters are in red. Others in blue." I wasn't sure if he meant me as a starter or not.

As though he knew what I was thinking, he said, "Yes, Maxwell. You'll be a starter."

Liam jogged over to the bench, picked up two red jerseys, and threw me one. "Maybe he lifted your suspension."

I had one more game on the bench before I could play, but my fingers were crossed that Liam was right. All I wanted to do was play basketball.

Once the team had split into blue and red, Coach pointed to the side closest to the exits. "Blue team, you'll be defense." He then tossed the ball to Chase Stevens, who was wearing a red jersey. "You and Maxwell at the other end of the court. I want you guys to show me you know how to play this darn game."

Chase and I hustled down to inbound the ball. He'd been quiet during practice, not taunting me or giving me the stink eye. In fact, he'd been keeping to himself, which made me scratch my head. We hated each other. He was the reason why Coach had benched me for three games.

I studied my enemy.

He bounced the ball, his expression devoid of any emotion, which was a stark contrast to when I'd first met him when he was loud and proud and a bully like his sister, Tessa.

"Remember, Maiken," Tessa said behind me. "We're meeting after practice."

I clenched my teeth at the sound of her voice. All she wanted to do was steal me away from Quinn. I wouldn't be surprised if the fundraiser she kept gabbing about was all a hoax to get my attention.

The cheerleaders giggled.

Chase glanced past me to his sister. "Why am I not surprised you picked him for your fundraiser team?"

And the Chase Stevens I knew was back—patronizing, loathing, and irritating. At least I felt like I was in the right place, because for a moment, I hadn't been sure.

Despite Chase, I wasn't about to acknowledge his sister even though the tension in me was ready to snap.

"Shut it, brother. I could give you shit about having the hots for pig girl."

Don't turn around. Don't spit at her. Don't even make a sound.

I was having a hard time refraining from doing something to shut her up, like stuff a sock in her mouth.

Chase stuck out his middle finger at his sister.

All that tension in me eased, and I grinned. Maybe he had some redeeming qualities after all. I knew he was defending Quinn's honor because he liked her, yet at the moment, I wanted to high-five him. He had my girl's back.

"Let's go," Coach shouted. "Stop gossiping down there."

Chase whipped the ball at me.

Catching it, I narrowed my eyes at him. "What the heck?"

He's mad at his sister, not you. In part, that was probably true.

"Just throw the ball in," he said with venom in his tone.

I hesitated for a split second to get the anger I was harboring under control because I was on the verge of throwing the ball at his head.

Once the ball was inbound, Chase jogged down to take up his position as shooting guard. He might've been jealous of me dating Quinn, but I was jealous that he'd gotten his way and could play shooting guard like he'd wanted. Coach had given me the position until Chase had thrown a temper tantrum. Yet in all fairness to Coach, he'd explained that Chase didn't have the skill to lead a team as a point guard, and Coach thought I did.

However, I'd never played point guard before, so I was learning the position as I went.

My basketball shoes squeaked along the wood floor as I dribbled down the court. Between the suicides and not sleeping well the night before, I swore I was a second away from passing out.

I waved off Phil Miller, our small forward, to get around his opponent.

"Pass the ball to me, Maxwell," Chase hollered at the top of his lungs, waving his arms as though he were stranded at sea.

"Get open, then." My voice echoed through the gym. All Chase did was hang under the net, giving me no opportunity to pass the ball to him since our zone defense was doing their job.

Liam held out his hands, free as a bird.

I was about to pass the ball to him when Coach's whistle trilled. "Everyone stop and don't move." He stomped out to midcourt, scowling. "What in the world is going on? Have you boys forgotten how to play the game? Miller, you should be moving your ass more under the basket, not hiding behind Rich. Chase, why are your feet glued to the floor? Maxwell, look at Woods. He's wide open."

So was Liam, but I dared not argue with Coach. I wanted to play this season, not sit on the bench.

Coach pulled the ball away from me then tossed it to one of three freshmen sitting on the sidelines. "All of you, find a seat on the bleachers."

Coach Dean could be rather scary when he spoke, even more so when his temper flared. He wanted to win games. He wanted us to work seamlessly as a team. I wanted all that too. I wanted scouts to watch me play well. I wanted a basketball scholarship to a good school like Ohio State or my dad's alma mater, UCLA, which were two of the top three on my list. But I wouldn't get noticed as a great player if I couldn't grasp the point guard position or if I kept throwing punches at Chase during games.

The ten of us found spots on the bleachers. I settled in the second row.

Liam joined me on my right, shoving his fingers through his sweat-soaked hair. "I have a feeling Coach is going to bring out the big guns."

Coach paced in front of us. I swore steam was billowing out of his ball cap.

I scanned the stands across from us. Only one boy and girl remained, and there was still no sign of Quinn. I assumed she would've shown up by then since Liam was her ride home.

Coach tucked his hands into the pockets of his khakis and seemed to glare at me. "I've made a decision."

My stomach knotted even though I hadn't done anything wrong, except for the two failing grades I had in English and chemistry.

Coach pulled off his ball cap, scratched his head, then put his hat back on. "This team sucks. I don't see us winning any games. You're horrible. The game is about teamwork. It's about fluidity of the plays. It's about getting into a position where Maxwell can pass the ball to you. It's not about who scores the most points. It's not about one individual. One of you screws up, everyone screws up." He flattened his lips into a thin line.

Liam leaned his elbows on his knees. "So what's your decision?"

"For the next month," Coach began, "we'll spend one day a week doing something outside of school hours as a team."

"I vote for skiing," Chase offered.

"Or shooting at the gun club," Miller said.

Coach chuckled, and it sounded as though whatever he had in mind wouldn't be something we were going to enjoy. "All of you will meet me at the Thompson farm at five a.m. tomorrow."

Chase reared back. "What? You want us to clean up shit?"

Liam growled low as he slapped Chase on the back of the head.

"Hey," Chase said. "It's your farm, not mine."

The rest of the team were shaking their heads.

I kept my mouth shut. I'd helped Quinn with chores, although horses weren't my thing. Regardless, I would get to see Quinn, and I chalked that up as a win. No better way to start my day.

"Do you know anything about this?" I asked Liam in a low voice.

"Not a clue."

"I can tell you right now, Coach," Chase continued. "I'm not working on a farm."

"It might do you some good," Liam said in a deep, hard tone. "It might put life into perspective for you instead of getting things handed to you on a silver platter."

Chase pushed Liam, who in turn fell into me.

Liam stood, ready to beat Chase to a pulp.

Coach wagged his finger at us. "Sit down, Thompson. This is what I'm talking about. None of you can get along."

"We did when Alex was here," Woods, who sat directly in front of me, said.

Coach's eyebrows rose. "You're right, Rich. I think it's time to elect a team captain."

I hadn't thought about a captain, but word from the guys was that Alex had been a great one, keeping everyone in line. I wasn't ready for that role and wasn't sure I wanted to lead a team yet.

Besides, captains didn't kill their teammates—something I would do to Chase Stevens.

Coach scrubbed a hand over his chin. "We'll vote at practice on Thursday. So between now and then, think about who you would like to see as your captain. And of course, as most of you know, I have the final say. Also, practice is canceled tomorrow and Wednesday. I have some personal business after school. We'll make up for lost time on Thursday, Friday, and Saturday to get ready for our game on Monday."

I leaned into Liam. "I vote for you." Liam would be the perfect person for the job. Like his brother, Carter, he didn't take shit from anyone, and people listened to him.

The loud squeak from the exit door made me turn my head. Basketball took a back seat when I laid eyes on my girl. She glided in like an angel, her long hair spilling down her chest, her sweater hugging her in all the right places, and her big smile that was only for me.

When she tucked her hair behind her ear, I was ready to jump off the bleachers. I desperately wanted to be that hand and feel her silky hair run through my fingers.

My brother Ethan thought it was funny that I'd brooded the entire time I was in Georgia. My feelings for Quinn made me understand why Ethan had sulked when we'd moved to Ashford and he'd had to leave his now ex-girlfriend behind.

Liam nudged me out of my reverie. "Stop drooling over my sister. It's not cool."

I smirked. I didn't care how it looked. Quinn was my girl, and brother or not, he wasn't going to stop me from looking.

Quinn climbed the bleachers with Celia not far behind. I hadn't noticed Celia before.

Liam elbowed me.

I smiled at my girl then turned my focus back to Coach.

"A final word about tomorrow before I let the cheerleaders speak. If one of you doesn't show or is late tomorrow morning, then all of you will pay the price."

"What will we be doing?" I asked.

Coach Dean picked up his clipboard. "I'll explain everything tomorrow. But make sure you're wearing boots."

Chase sneered. "You'll be getting a call from my dad, Coach."

"I have his approval," Coach said with satisfaction in his tone.

Chase sucked in a sharp breath.

I grinned, enjoying every minute of the hell Chase was in.

Liam slapped Chase on the shoulder. "I'll make sure you're with the pigs."

Chase groaned.

Coach waved the cheerleaders over.

I stiffened as I sat up straighter.

The squad hurried over with smiles all around. The only girl that stood out in height was a redhead who was about four inches taller than her counterparts.

"Brianna," Coach said. "Please explain what the fundraiser is all about this year."

Brianna Masters was petite, and her long brown hair was tied up in a ponytail. She was pretty but wore too much makeup for me. As she spoke, she fidgeted with credit cards in her hands. "Hey, guys. For this year's fundraiser, we'll be going door to door, selling these cards for twenty dollars. On the card are discounts to places like Shakers, the ice-skating rink, and other local businesses in town."

"Her dad owns the ice-skating rink," Liam said.

I gave him a sidelong glance. "And that should excite me why?"

"No reason. My brother Carter has a thing for her, though."

Brianna continued. "On Saturday afternoon, you'll be paired with a cheerleader to sell twenty-five cards. And with thirteen teams of two, we could raise $6,500 that will fund our away games and other necessary expenses for the sports program."

"What if we don't sell all the cards?" Liam asked. "Are we doing this every day until we can?"

"Let's start with Saturday," Brianna said.

"Why not set up a table at the home game on Monday and sell them?" Chase offered.

Tessa stepped out of formation. "We'll have them available at the refreshment stand, but we won't sell all of them at the game." Her gaze was cemented to me.

Suddenly, I felt like I needed a shower.

"I'm not partnering with Tessa," I said as low as I could to Liam.

"If you want to be a team player, you really don't have a choice," he fired back.

I gritted my teeth. "We all have choices." But I knew if I didn't participate, Coach would have my hide.

Coach cleared his throat. "The cheerleaders have everyone paired up, and everyone will participate." He emphasized those last two words.

Liam snickered. "No getting out of it, Maxwell."

I threw my head in my hands as Brianna listed off the pairs. When she said my name alongside Tessa's, I wanted to puke. I dared not look at Quinn, afraid if I did, I would find sadness written all over her. And that would devastate me.

Chapter 3

Quinn

Anger burned every nerve ending in me as I ground my back teeth together. I wanted to protest and tell Coach that Tessa and Maiken weren't working together, but then I would only be like Tessa—crying about something I didn't like. That wasn't me. Daddy had taught me a long time ago that sometimes I had to accept things that were out of my control. Besides, I couldn't cry about a fundraiser for the school. In spite of that, I would think of something to make sure Tessa didn't get her grubby hands on Maiken.

"Brianna and Liam," Celia said almost to herself. Celia had a thing for my brother, and her tone screamed jealousy. But I didn't think Brianna had any interest in Liam. Like Tessa, Brianna could be a snob, though rumor around school was that Brianna had changed since her boyfriend, Alex Baker, had died.

Coach Dean left, as did most of the cheerleaders, basketball team, and spectators, leaving Tessa, who climbed the bleachers to sit next to Maiken. Brianna cornered Liam as he stepped down. Chase picked at a nail, coyly watching his sister. Celia kept Liam in her sights. I sat rigid, watching, thinking, and silently screaming.

Maiken finally removed his hands from his face and peeked my way. His eyes pleaded with me to help him out.

That was all I needed to kick myself into high gear. I popped up like a jack-in-the-box, grabbed the plastic bag of Tessa's clothes I'd borrowed from her that night of her party, and stormed across the shiny wood floor. Hurried footsteps pounded behind me as Celia trailed. Nerves coiled in the pit of my stomach as the bag in my hand trembled.

Maiken met me at center court, and Tessa followed him at breakneck speed.

Liam, Brianna, and Chase came over as though they were a security detail about to prevent a brawl.

All of us were in somewhat of a circle with Maiken at my side. He seemed to be watching me, maybe because I was breathing fire.

"Sis," Liam said. "Are you okay?"

Not in the least. Images of Tessa and me pulling out each other's hair flashed before my eyes.

Swallowing my nerves, I dug deep for the courage to say something. I was afraid to open my mouth, though. With my luck, I would stutter or spout off some fact about hussies and harridans.

Tessa fisted her hands at her side, ready to take me on, much like I'd done that morning when I approached her in the hall.

"Tessa." Brianna's soprano voice snapped one cord of tension. "Remember the rules. No fighting, or you'll be suspended from the squad."

Suddenly, Momma's words about trouble and not dating Maiken blared in my head.

Those fisted hands at Tessa's side loosened. "You know I don't physically fight."

I rolled my eyes. "There's a first for everything." I silently high-fived myself for not stuttering.

Chase grinned. "I'm digging your spunk, Quinn."

Tessa huffed. "Chase, why don't you just kiss her already and be done with it."

Shooting daggers at Chase, Maiken draped his arm around me and tugged me to him. His body was warm and strong, and we fit together so well. In that moment, I felt like I could do anything.

Chase considered Maiken then me. "I think it's time we go home, Tessa."

Maiken's jaw hit the floor. Even my brother had shock written all over his sweaty face.

I was partly surprised Chase hadn't said something snarky to his sister or to Maiken when he'd pulled me to him.

I jutted out my chin and handed the plastic bag to Tessa. "Here's your clothes." My voice was laced with all kinds of sugar. "Remember? The ones I'd borrowed at your holiday party."

Kill them with kindness was something Momma would say often when a mean customer in the farm store confronted her.

Tessa swatted my hand. "I told you to burn them."

The bag fell to the floor.

Walk away. Don't cry. You're better than her.

I wasn't sure about the latter. I wanted to hit her as much as she wanted to hurt me. So I was no better than her.

Taking in a breath, I searched every nook and cranny in me for patience more than confidence. "Why are you so m-mean?"

I'd read up on bullying, and some of the reasons bullies lashed out were stress, abuse, insecurity, and jealousy. The one I could pin on Tessa was insecurity, which I didn't understand. She was pretty, she was popular, and she had a beautiful home and loving family. Regardless, I couldn't figure out how her insecurity related to hating me.

Brianna flashed her brown gaze at Tessa. I had a feeling she was waiting for a reason to kick Tessa off the squad.

Chase picked up the bag of clothes. "She's just jealous of you, Quinn."

I did a double take. I lived on a farm, had my nose in books most of the time, and wasn't popular in the least. Surely she couldn't be envious of all that. Then again, if anyone knew the real reason why Tessa had it out for me, it was her brother.

Tessa's cheeks flamed red. "Shut up!"

"Oh my God," Celia said. "That makes total sense. You've always hated when teachers put Quinn up on a pedestal for her grades or always having the right answers in class. And now that she's dating Maiken, your jealousy is off the charts because she won the boy. You can't accept that Maiken doesn't want you."

Maiken squeezed me to him as though making it very clear to everyone that we were boyfriend and girlfriend and no one would tear us apart.

I snuck a peek at Chase to see how he was taking all this since he'd made his intentions known that he liked me. Not that long ago, he'd been determined to win me over before Maiken and I had become an item. I didn't want him to steal me away from Maiken. The Chase I knew was much like his sister—determined, a bully, and he didn't take no for an answer. Yet the Chase I was looking at now had a blank expression. He seemed more reserved and seemed to be shying away from confrontation.

Fury darkened Tessa's complexion even more. "I don't have time for this. I have skating practice tonight."

Brianna licked her red lips, and her eyes flicked between Tessa and me. "You two aren't leaving this gym until you air out your differences." She sounded as though she were the adult among us. Granted, she was a senior. But she was visibly irritated with Tessa more than me.

"I agree," Liam piped in. He'd been watching things unfold

without interfering, which was new for my brother. Normally, he would've told Tessa to back off a long time ago.

Regardless, I could feel my eyes bulging out of my head. Liam didn't do interventions.

Tessa planted her hands on her hips as she sneered at her head cheerleader. "You're not the boss of me."

Brianna, who was Tessa's height, glared at her teammate. "I am while you're on my squad."

Tessa and Brianna were in a staredown.

I would be glad to work out things with Tessa if I knew she would change. But Tessa Stevens didn't understand what the word change meant. She was born with hatred in her bones.

Nevertheless, I had to do my part, whatever that part was. And if it didn't work, at least I could say I tried. "I'm all for settling our differences before we walk out the door."

Tessa snorted. "Such the goody two-shoes. Give me a break. I'm out of here. I only have the rink for an hour tonight."

"What if we settle things on the ice?" I blurted out. I was probably going to regret that, but it would level the battlefield. She skated. I skated. Maybe we could settle our differences on the ice. That way, no one got hurt. No one had to throw a punch or pull out hair. Besides, it might be fun to see if I could beat her at the sport—something I hadn't done even though I'd tried for years.

You're rusty. She's not. But I could practice. Again, I had to try something. I didn't want to spend the rest of my high school years dealing with her.

All heads rounded to me. I glanced up at Maiken, who was grinning and nodding.

Tessa crossed her arms over her chest. "You want to do a skate-off? Ha! You'll lose. You know that."

All I did was shrug. She didn't need to know that I'd been skating on the lake for the last couple of months.

"Who says she'll lose?" Celia piped in.

Brianna clapped. "I think a skate-off is a brilliant idea."

Celia and Brianna were sending me good vibes, although my heart was hammering in my chest. "If I win, then we call a truce."

Chase, Maiken, and Liam were quiet.

Tessa studied me. "For real? You won't win." Her confident tone belied the stiffness in her jaw.

Given the statistics of her record versus mine, I would have to agree with her.

"Then w-why do you look scared?" I asked.

"She can so beat you." Maiken's Southern drawl, which I realized was thicker than when I'd first met him, blanketed my body in tingles.

Tessa pushed out a shoulder. "She can't. But hey, I'll take that bet."

Brianna cleared her throat. "Good. It's settled. Celia and I will line up some judges, and I'll check with my dad on when we could schedule ice time at the rink for the competition."

Celia nodded in agreement. "Sounds good."

The word competition did something to my insides. They felt as if they were going through the spin cycle in a washing machine. Now I needed to focus on practicing for sure.

"All I have to say is if I win, you better be prepared for hell." Then Tessa stomped off.

Before Chase followed his sister, he said, "You got this."

I let out all the air in my lungs.

"To keep things fair," Brianna said, "I'll make sure you get some ice time at the rink to practice."

I reared back, surprised she was helping me. The rumors were true, then. She was a nicer person. "I don't have the money." Renting an hour of time at the rink was expensive.

"I do," Maiken said.

My eyes went wide as happy tears threatened. But I couldn't take his money. Nevertheless, my heart exploded with joy.

"We'll all pitch in," Liam said.

"Not necessary," Brianna added. "We'll charge a cover fee, which will pay for the ice time. We'll afford the same free ice time to Tessa to keep things fair."

She made it hard for me to protest. "Thank you."

"We'll be in touch," Brianna said to Celia and me. Then she walked out.

Celia squealed. "It's on. Time to get your blades sharpened."

"I'm proud of you, sis," Liam said. "You didn't resort to punching Tessa, although I would've enjoyed that too."

"Believe me, I was a second away from pushing her on her butt," I said.

Maiken removed his arm from around my shoulder. "What stopped you?"

I almost pouted at the loss of his touch. "I know this sounds crazy. But I felt sorry for her when her own brother threw her under the bus." That was the truth. Sure, I had other reasons too, but I did feel sorry that her own blood relative hadn't stuck up for her.

"Well, this should be epic." Celia's voice hitched. "And you so got this."

Liam went over to the bleachers and snagged his sweatshirt. "Quinn, we should get home. I need to change first. I'll meet you at the car." Then he wandered off.

"Wait," Celia called as she scurried up to him. "Quinn, see you tomorrow."

Maiken flicked his head at the exit. "I need to go too. Kade is picking me up."

I knitted my eyebrows. "Kade? You don't have your car?"

He grabbed his hoodie from the bleachers. "I'm staying with him and Lacey. My aunt Denise is having some medical tests done this week, and my mom felt that she needed to stay a few extra days. They should be home at the end of the week." Sadness weaved through every word.

"Is your aunt okay?"

He pulled his hoodie over his head. "Not sure."

My chest tightened. He didn't need any more bad news in his family. But any questions I had about his aunt were forgotten when he sauntered over to me with a sense of purpose and a mischievous grin.

I sucked in a breath when his gaze dropped to my lips. Then before I could blink, he was dragging the pad of his thumb over my mouth. "I want you to know that there's one thing Tessa will never win."

Goose bumps fired along my arms at the huskiness in his tone.

"She'll never get me." Then his lips crashed against mine.

I became a cooked noodle, forgetting about Tessa, skating, winning, and anything else around us.

Chapter 4

Maiken

Miller, Woods, Liam, and I huddled inside the horse barn at the Thompson farm, waiting on Chase. The rest of the basketball team was in another barn with the cows and their drill sergeant, who was none other than Carter Thompson, Liam's older brother.

The four us fidgeted on our booted feet, with our hands jammed in our pockets. Knit hats covered our heads, and steam came out of our mouths as the cold, cold morning seeped into our bones.

The horses didn't seem to mind, though. A couple of them nickered as their heads poked out of the stalls, seemingly looking at the bales of hay that lined the center of the aisle outside the stalls.

"The only thing keeping me awake," Woods said, sniffling, "is the awful scent of manure."

Liam busted out laughing. "It's mild this morning with the wind blowing in."

Woods pulled down his hat to cover more of his blond hair and big ears. "Chase better show."

Yawning, I shuffled on my feet, nodding. Sleep had escaped me for a second night in a row, and I'd found myself lying in bed, staring at the popcorn ceiling in the guest room at Lacey's dad's house.

I'd spoken to my mom before bed, and she had sounded extremely worried about her sister. She wouldn't tell me what was going on even though I'd tried to pull it out of her.

"You don't need anything else to take your mind off of school. You kids have been through enough with your dad passing."

She didn't need anything else either.

Coach, who was talking to Mr. Thompson near Apple's stall, glanced at his watch.

I did the same. Chase had three minutes before the clock struck five. I couldn't imagine what was in store for us if he didn't show or was even one minute late.

"So what are we doing this morning?" I asked Liam even though it wasn't hard to figure out that we would be working around the horses. I wasn't as afraid of them since I'd been around Apple a few times when I'd helped Quinn with her chores. "Is Quinn joining us this morning?" Her presence would make my morning, for sure.

Liam blew into his hands. "Probably not, dude. My dad told her she could take the morning off."

Miller, the shorter of us four, shifted from one foot to the other, wiping his nose with the back of his hand. "I will kill Chase if he doesn't show." His green eyes watered, probably from the cold wind that swept in.

I was with him. But Chase had no desire to get kicked off the team. That much I was certain of.

Footsteps pounded toward the horse barn, and we heard a guy breathing heavily. We all turned to find Carter, Liam's older brother.

Carter's face was pinched, looking as mean as ever. "Why are you all standing around?"

"Waiting on Chase," Liam said.

Carter plucked a beanie out of the back pocket of his jeans and pulled it over his brown head of hair. "Fuck Chase. We got to get this shit done before school starts."

"Tell that to Coach," I said snidely.

Carter was one Thompson who rubbed me the wrong way. He'd been overly protective of Quinn when I'd first met her, going as far as making my life hell when a rumor went around school that Quinn and I had slept together. I couldn't blame him for protecting his sister. I would do the same for any of my sisters. But in my mind, he was way over the top.

Carter blew past us and over to his dad.

"Normally, we would have most of the stalls done by now," Liam said.

Coach zipped up his jacket. "It seems Chase doesn't want to play basketball."

Inwardly, I was jumping up and down for joy because that meant I could play shooting guard.

But my excitement was short-lived.

"I'm here," Chase yelled as he rushed up to us.

Coach's jaw turned to stone. "Do you like pissing off your team-mates? Or me for that matter?"

"Coach—" Chase started.

Coach held up his gloved hand. "When I say to be on time, I mean it. Now where are your boots?"

Chase briefly lowered his gaze to his white tennis shoes. "That's the problem, Coach. I was looking for them for the last hour."

Steam floated out of Coach's nose. "No excuse. You'll follow everything Carter tells you to do. You'll work in twos. Woods, you're with Carter. Miller and Liam. And yes"—Coach started to grin—"Maxwell and Stevens. Maybe working together will do you two some good."

Cuss words rang in my head.

Carter stabbed a finger at the high bench by the door. "Get gloves. Then take a stall, clean out the shit, replace the horse's bedding with the hay you see in the aisle, and fill their buckets with food and water. We have seven stalls. When you're done with yours, move on to the next one. Are we clear?"

Carter would do well as a military leader. In fact, as much as I wasn't a Carter fan, my dad would've loved him.

Chase raised his hand. "Where do we dump the crap?"

"One of the three wheelbarrows you see in the aisle," Mr. Thompson said.

Hustling to get a pair of gloves, I spotted Quinn walking toward us. Her hair was up in a high ponytail, she wore furry earmuffs around her ears, and she was dressed in jeans, an oversized hoodie, and rubber boots that climbed up to her knees.

Mr. Thompson followed my line of sight. "Sweet girl, I told you to sleep in."

She gave her dad one of her award-winning smiles. "I know. But we have a lot of chores to do. Someone has to feed the cows and the rest of the animals."

He kissed her on the forehead. "Don't think I don't know why you're down here."

Chase slapped me on the arm. "Move, asswipe. You don't want Carter up your butt. Do you?"

As much as I wanted to stare at Quinn or do more than stare, my enemy was right. I slipped on my gloves and started for Apple's stall, only to find Liam and Miller working in there.

Well, crap. I was comfortable with Apple.

When Chase and I looked in the next stall, we both glanced at each other then at the black stallion who was bigger than Apple and so much scarier.

"You want to go in first?" Chase asked.

That was a big, fat no. I grabbed the shovel that sat outside the stall. "Here. You shovel. I'll get a wheelbarrow."

"Like hell," Chase whined. "You pick up the shit."

Quinn bounced up. "Now, boys. Oscar is harmless." She zipped into the stall, talking to Oscar like she was talking to a dog.

Chase ran in. "Oscar, huh?"

I rolled my eyes and clenched my back teeth before going in.

"See?" Quinn singsonged. "Oscar is a big teddy bear."

Chase didn't get too close, which surprised me. I recalled the day he'd shown up at the tree farm when Quinn had been riding Apple. He hadn't been afraid at all.

"So you don't like horses, man?" I asked.

"I'm cool," he said, not taking his eyes off of Quinn... or maybe Oscar.

"Yeah, right," I mumbled.

Quinn kept petting Oscar around the nose. "You boys should get started. My dad doesn't like slackers."

You mean Carter doesn't.

Lo and behold, Carter poked his head in. "Idiots, the shit isn't going to clean itself." Then he noticed Quinn. "Sis, can I have a word?"

She giggled before turning around. "I was just leaving." As she left the stall, her hand brushed mine, and electricity zapped up my arm.

Maybe that was all I needed because I grabbed the shovel. "Get the wheelbarrow, man."

Chase kicked into gear at my command. I chuckled at how he ran out faster than a racing horse.

Quinn returned and glanced over the stall. "Maiken, are you going to be okay with Oscar?"

I was standing two feet away from a very large horse, which was nerve-racking, and my stomach was twisting. But I had to face my fear and show Quinn I wasn't that much of a pansy. Besides, I wasn't about to make a fool of myself in front of her, Chase, and the guys.

"I got this," I said.

Oscar nickered as though he agreed with me.

Quinn's amber eyes sparkled in the bright lights of the barn. "I'll see you later, then."

Chase came in with the wheelbarrow as Quinn disappeared from view. "So you're afraid of horses? Wimp ass."

Ignore him.

He muttered something else I couldn't make out.

"Look, can the barbs." *Or else I'll throw you onto this pile of manure that's burning my nostrils.*

He sneered. "Fuck off."

Biting my tongue, I scooped a shovel full of Oscar's shit, preparing to dump it into the wheelbarrow that Chase was holding on to for dear life.

He looked at the shovel then back at me. "You wouldn't dare."

It took me a second to realize he thought I was going to throw the shit at him. As much as I would've liked to have seen his bright-white sneakers dirty with manure, it was best we didn't fight around a horse. If we spooked Oscar, the outcome would not be good for Chase or me.

Nevertheless, I flung the shovel over the wheelbarrow a little too quick and hard, causing some of the manure to hit the edge of the steel bed near Chase's hands. Some of the manure ended up falling out onto Chase's jeans and white sneakers.

He growled. "What the fuck, man? You did that on purpose."

Honestly, it was an accident. "Then step away from the wheelbarrow."

Coach peered over the stall. "What's going on?"

"Nothing," Chase said.

"Yeah. We're cool." We were far from cool.

Mr. Thompson sidled up to Coach. "Stevens, why are you standing around? Grab the damn hose and fill Oscar's water bucket." Mr. Thompson's tone permitted no argument.

Chase narrowed his eyes at me before banging his foot against the wheelbarrow to rid his clean white shoes of shit.

I held in the urge to roar with laughter.

Coach Dean folded his bulky arms over his chest. "I guess I have to watch you two."

"Send them over every morning," Mr. Thompson said. "I'll break them."

Chase and I both froze. I wasn't afraid of hard work, and I didn't need breaking as though I were one of Mr. Thompson's horses. But I wasn't about to talk back. My dad had taught me to mind my elders.

"That's a great idea," Coach added.

As though Coach and Mr. Thompson had scared us straight, Chase and I went to work filling water buckets, shoveling manure, and replacing part of Oscar's bedding, all under the keen eye of Coach.

An hour and a half later, all the stalls were clean, the horses were fed, and I was exhausted. Maybe after a morning or two like this, I would be able to sleep.

The basketball team gathered outside the barn—dirty, stinky, and tired—waiting for Coach to get off the phone.

No one was saying a word, but several yawned—me included.

I was fighting to keep my eyes open as I blinked several times, staring out at the oranges and purples streaking the horizon as the sun started to rise. On another blink, I scanned the farm for Quinn but came up empty.

"I am not doing this again tomorrow," Chase muttered next to me.

I couldn't help but laugh. Like the rest of us, he was covered in shit, dirt, and hay from head to toe. But what had me in stitches was how his white sneakers were now as brown as his hair.

"Shut the fuck up, Maxwell," Chase said. "You look as bad as the rest of us."

I brought my hand to my mouth. "Sure. But those pearly whites on your feet are disgusting."

The rest of the guys snickered.

Coach pocketed his phone. "Listen up." He surveyed each of us like he was a military commander inspecting his troops. "Any of you learn anything today?"

"I'm not doing this again," Chase said.

I winced. The asshat was going to get all of us in trouble.

Coach scraped a hand over his chin. "Is that right?" He inched up to Chase and stood toe to toe. "I am sick and tired of your poor attitude. Since Alex died, you have been one cranky player. You don't listen anymore. Your team skills went out the window, and you feel Maxwell is out to get you."

A muscle jumped along Chase's jaw. "Shoveling crap isn't showing us how to work as a team."

Coach's face turned beet red. "See, that's your problem. How can you learn anything when you're always mouthing off? You can't even shovel shit without arguing with Maxwell."

Chase pushed a thumb at me. "It was his fault."

"It was an accident," I mumbled.

"Can it," Coach said to me as he stepped back. "Miller, what did you learn in the last hour?"

Miller flicked black hair out of his eyes. "Respect, Coach."

"Woods, how about you?" Coach asked.

"That Liam should get a medal for doing this every day," Woods said.

Coach turned to me. "Maxwell?"

"Aside from respect for the Thompsons, that I'll do whatever it takes to get our team on the right track." I wasn't going to let Chase get the best of me either.

Coach studied me before he said, "Good to hear. Chase, you want to add anything?"

Chase cast his gaze downward.

Coach began pacing, pinning a look on each player as he did. "Look, colleges aren't going to be interested in any of you if you can't show them team skills. You can shoot all the three-pointers or score the most points in a game, but if they don't see team skills, then they'll look at someone else. We're done here. And for Chase being late, we'll meet here again tomorrow morning, same time."

Chase stormed off like he always did when he didn't get his way, or maybe Coach had hit a nerve with him.

Coach certainly had with me. I wanted scouts to notice me. The problem was that they wouldn't unless all of us were in sync and seamless in our plays—fluid as Coach had said.

I knew what I had to do. Hopefully Chase did as well.

Chapter 5

Quinn

Our legs dangled over the edge of the barn's loft door as Maiken and I looked out at the rolling hills of the farm. Silence shrouded us as though we were both wrestling with our inner demons.

School had been crazy that day with word bouncing through the halls about Tessa and me competing on the ice. Celia, who was now officially on the school's newspaper, was writing an article about the big event.

"It will draw more kids in, which means more money," she'd said.

The more people talked about it, the more I wanted to puke. By the time we had the skate-off, I wouldn't have any nerves left, let alone be able to skate.

I slid my hand over to Maiken's, which was warm yet cold. "Are you okay?" I knew he was worried about his aunt Denise, but I hadn't had a chance to ask him more about her or why he'd returned to Ashford and his siblings hadn't. "Any more news on your aunt?"

He interlaced his calloused fingers with mine. "Nothing yet." He released a sigh. "It's pretty up here."

This was my peaceful place for sure. Streaks of orange and bluish-purples streaked the horizon as though a painter had taken his brush, dipped it into a mixture of colored paints, and swiped it one way then the other. The beauty of the scene, though, was how the snow-covered hills of the farm made the horizon pop even brighter as dusk set in.

"So why were you the only one to return?" Eleanor and Martin were on vacation, so I suspected that had something to do with his brothers and sisters staying behind.

"My mom didn't want me to miss basketball, and honestly, I'm failing two classes."

Yikes! I recalled Emma saying something about how Maiken wanted to go into the NBA, but first he had to get into college, and that meant he had to get good grades.

"Does Coach know?" I knew Carter had been sidelined from football in his junior year because of his grade in history.

Maiken pushed out his shoulders. "Not sure."

I was sure Coach would find out. "I can help you if you want." I'd tutored a couple of people in my freshman year when I'd worked in the math lab.

A twinkle lit his eye. "Do you think we would get any studying done?"

Probably not. "Sure." If it meant he could play basketball, I would do whatever I could to help him.

He laughed. "I'm good. I just need to study more."

We held hands as silence, uncomfortable in one sense and perfect in another, stretched between us. I itched to say or do something, anything to make him smile. Yet sometimes a person just needed a hand to hold, a hand that said "I'm here for you."

He began rubbing my finger with his thumb, and a slow grin emerged as he peeked at me.

Suddenly, I had visions of us rolling around on the hay-strewn floor behind us, kissing until we both needed air. "Did you know that the most important m-muscle in kissing is the orbicularis oris? It allows the lips to pucker."

He gave me his full attention, flashing a bright-white smile that morphed into a belly laugh. "Where do you get all these facts?"

And just like that, the tension-filled air blew away with the cold wind.

I tittered. "I want to be a doctor. So I read a lot about the human anatomy."

He batted the long lashes framing his yummy blue eyes. "Wow, a doctor."

"Have you thought about college?" I asked.

Stupid girl. Don't change the subject from kissing to college.

"Sure. I want to play college ball, but as far as a major, I don't have one ironed out yet. I've thought of going into the military too." He returned his attention to the waning blue sky. "My mom might not be cool with it."

I knew my mom wouldn't be excited about any of us going into the military. I wasn't sure about Daddy. Then again, Carter hadn't decided yet if he was going to college. Liam, on the other hand, wanted to play basketball for Georgetown.

For a long minute, an awkward silence took over until a crisp, cold breeze swept in.

Then Maiken flinched before he leaned back on his elbows. "Do you have any advice for me in working with Tessa on Saturday?"

Run. Run. Run.

I had to swivel my neck to look at him. "Is that what's been bothering you?"

"Partly."

I shivered when another hard wind blew in, so I scooted back until I was sitting up against a bale of hay.

Maiken popped up, closed the loft door, then blew into his hands.

I picked up a straw of hay. "I have an idea that might help you with Tessa."

Eager, he sat down facing me. "I'm all ears." His raspy voice caused my belly to go haywire. Or maybe I had that reaction because his gaze was riveted on my lips.

I looked away as heat crawled up my neck. "First, you have to kiss me." My mouth got ahead of my brain, but in that one instant, I didn't scold myself. A kiss for an answer sounded like a good bargain.

He toyed with the laces on my boots. "Are you bribing me, Quinn Thompson?"

My chin angled down and away as I batted my lashes. "Maybe."

He roughed a hand through his thick sandy-blond hair as he kicked out his long, muscular legs on either side of me. Then he took both my hands in his. "Come here."

He didn't have to tell me twice. I adjusted my body, crossing my legs underneath me, and got as close to him as I could.

He grinned as big as the Atlantic Ocean.

Oh my! I was in trouble.

Still eyeing my lips as though they were his favorite candy, Maiken asked, "Why are you so pretty?"

I moistened my lips. "Th-that's not a fair question."

"That's not an answer. Try again."

I playfully swatted at his denim-clad thigh. "Genetics, I guess."

"Mm. You do look a little like your mom, and she's sort of hot."

My face twisted. "You think my mom is hot?" She was pretty, but hearing him say *hot* and *my mom* sounded weird on so many levels.

"She's as pretty as you."

I knotted my hands in my lap as fire flooded my cheeks. My

pulse was all over the place, even more so when he lifted my chin with his fingers.

"You're beautiful, Quinn," he said in his Southern drawl.

Goose bumps popped up, quick and fast, all over me. And if he kept looking at me with his eyes hooded and a grin that was all naughty and nice, I might be forward enough to tackle him to the ground and kiss him until I couldn't breathe.

Slowly, tentatively, he leaned forward so that his lips were a hairbreadth from mine. "Is it okay if I kiss you now?"

I tried to speak, but my tongue was dormant and as dry as a desert. I swished the saliva around in my mouth in an attempt to get my muscles working. But before I could, he stuck his tongue in my mouth. He tasted like lime and mint, and I was in heaven, flying around the stars, the moon, and the planets. This boy had a way of making me forget all my worries and fears. He had a way of bringing me out of my shell. He had a way of touching my heart with such emotion that I was falling hard and fast for him.

We kissed for a long minute, his tongue and mine knotting, dancing, and just plain learning. We were both new at kissing, and I loved the fact that we were learning together. I loved that this was his first relationship and mine, and I hoped that maybe it would turn into more as time went on.

He broke the kiss and squirmed a bit. I didn't have to look down in between us to know he was adjusting himself. He'd gotten an erection during our first kiss in the boathouse. Boys' reactions were visible and could be embarrassing, but he grinned, and I smiled. His phallus —or boner, as my brothers would say—didn't matter . I was having all kinds of reactions too. I was sure my cheeks were as red as a ripe tomato from our vegetable garden.

"So what's your idea?" His voice was hoarse.

I puffed out my cheeks, trying to get my body, heart, and mind to calm down. As soon as I thought of Tessa, my body instantly cooled. "My grandmother has her monthly poker game at her house with a bunch of her friends on Saturday. They'll buy the cards, or most of them anyway, then we could sell the rest at the farm store." That way, he wouldn't have to spend that much time with Tessa, and I wouldn't fret about it for the entire day.

"I'm game."

I didn't think Tessa would be, but I didn't care. Maiken was my boyfriend, and she wasn't getting her grubby little hands on him if I could help it.

He latched on to a few strands of my hair that fell over my chest, his hand coming awfully close to my breasts. "You know she'll protest."

"So? It's about raising money, nothing more." Maybe the time the three of us spent together would make her see that Maiken didn't like her or that I wasn't as terrible as she thought I was.

Maiken shrugged. "Maybe after Chase calling her out yesterday, she might realize the error of her ways."

I laughed hard. "I doubt that." I couldn't imagine anything taking away Tessa's meanness.

"I can see why she's jealous of you," he said.

My breath hitched, and my hair fell over my eye as I tipped my head to one side.

Maiken tucked my hair behind my ear. "Don't be surprised by that. Did you know that Quinn means wisdom, reason, and intelligence? Add that to your prettiness, and any girl would be envious."

My jaw came unhinged while my heart bloomed, oozing warmth and so much more.

He'd researched my name.

As quick as the Flash, I tackled him to the floor, adjusting myself so I was sitting on top of him with my hands pressed to his chest. "Now *you're* spitting out facts?"

He gripped my hips. "I want to know who my girl really is."

My heart was galloping faster than my horse, Apple. "Who am I?"

He managed to sit up under my weight. "You're *my* girl."

If he continued to whisper words that made me gooey all over, like the sticky buns Granny made on Christmas, I didn't need any endorphins to kick-start my self-confidence. I had him.

Chapter 6

Maiken

The car ride to school was quiet as Kade drove. I'd busted my ass at the farm for the second morning in a row. The team had shown up on time, including Chase. Coach had thrown us together again, but Chase had been in his own little world, stewing over something that I didn't care to ask about.

I'd been in my own head, desperately wanting to know more about my aunt Denise. But I hadn't talked to Mom. Her text had said that she would call on Thursday night, but it was only Wednesday.

Kade braked at a stop sign and cleared his throat. "What's bothering you?"

I must have been wearing my feelings on my sleeve because Quinn kept asking me the same thing. I hadn't told her everything that was bothering me either. I didn't want to dump all my problems on her. She had enough on her plate with her upcoming competition with Tessa.

Piles of snow lined the streets of Ashford. Lacey and Kade lived close to downtown, and the only way to school was by way of Main Street.

Kade huffed out a breath. "Come on, man. I'm not oblivious. Is it Quinn? Are you having girl problems?"

Just hearing her name made me warm all over. The girl was worming her way into my heart, and while that frightened me, it also gave me a jolt of exhilaration. For some reason, I had a sinking feeling that my mom might not want to return. After all, we weren't tied down to any house or place, and she wanted to settle somewhere.

An older man entered a coffee shop as Kade navigated at a slow speed, approaching the next stop sign.

One beat then two passed before I said, "No. It's not Quinn." I was hesitant to unload on him. He had said I could talk to him, and in part, he reminded me of my dad. But I didn't know where to begin. So much weighed on me—my dad's death, my grades, basketball, my mom, Aunt Denise, and I missed my brothers and sisters.

Silence followed us for two blocks.

"How did you handle Karen's death?" I finally asked. Maybe he could give me some insight on how to work through my feelings.

He kept his gaze on the road. "Man, that is a loaded question."

"Sorry."

He grabbed the nape of his neck. "Don't be sorry. Death is hard to deal with, man. And you can't just get over the death of a loved one overnight. But I don't have an easy answer. All of us deal with death differently. For me, I was angry as all get out. Angry at Karen. Angry at her friend for pulling the trigger. Angry at my old man even though he had the gun safe locked down tight." A muscle ticked in his unshaven jaw. "It was a rough time for all of us." He rounded a corner down a side street. "One thing that helped me was celebrating her life rather than mourning her death."

The school loomed in the distance.

"How?"

"There are many ways, but my brothers and I set up a small memorial in the woods across the lake. We had her initials carved into a large stone rock with five hearts etched into it. She loved hearts. She always told us that a beating heart was the mystery behind a person." His Adam's apple bobbed. "I miss her so fucking much." He blew out a breath. "Find something to celebrate your dad." He touched his chest. "Keep him here with whatever you do."

"He loved basketball," I mumbled.

"Then play the game like you've never played it before, Maiken. Don't lash out in the middle of a game. Don't take your anger out on those who don't deserve it. Make your dad proud as though he were watching your game in the stands."

Kade had been at the game when I'd punched Chase. Regardless, tears were ready to spill. Maybe if I found a way to deal with my dad's death, then I could concentrate on school and basketball and not be so angry.

"I spoke to your mom last night," Kade said. "She told me that you're failing a couple of classes. She asked me to help you. Do you need help?"

I pushed out a shoulder. "Not yet. It's just a matter of me doing the work."

"Then until you get your grades up, you'll come home right after basketball practice and study every day."

I jerked my head his way, ready to protest. I knew what I had to do.

Then why haven't you done it?

He pinned me with a hard look that dared me to argue. "While you're living with Lacey and me, you're my responsibility. I promised your mom I would make sure you got your grades up and that you stuck with basketball. So are we clear?"

Whoa! I wasn't expecting that kind of discipline out of Kade, but like Coach, he could be rather intimidating.

"Yes." As much as I didn't like someone other than my parents telling me what to do, I was living with him, and I couldn't disappoint my mom.

Kade wheeled into the school lot and stopped at the curb in front of the main entrance. "Does Coach know about your grades?"

I grasped the handle of the door, ready to bolt. "No. Or if he does, he hasn't said anything to me." Report cards came out just before Christmas break, so I suspected Coach would find out soon enough if he didn't know already.

Kade nodded out the windshield. "You should tell him now."

Coach Dean was walking toward us. One hand was in his winter coat pocket, and the other was waving at us.

I wasn't ready to face the music that early in the morning. Nevertheless, I climbed out of the truck. *Here goes nothing.*

Coach grabbed the top of the car door. "Just the person I wanted to see."

For a second, I assumed he was talking to me until he bent down to regard Kade. "Can I have a word, Kade? I need your help with something."

"Sure," Kade said to Coach. "Let me park. Oh, and Maiken, remember what we talked about. I would recommend getting that done today."

I hiked my backpack over my shoulder then made my way into school, thinking about how I was going to break the news to Coach. But when I spotted Quinn talking with Celia, my grades didn't matter.

Quinn beamed up at me as though her day had been made.

Mine sure had. I drank in every inch of her, from the skinny jeans that accentuated her petite body to the way the jersey fabric of her shirt hugged her breasts. I didn't know if her clothes were new, but they were more formfitting than I remembered. But her curves weren't what had my stomach spinning and my pulse racing. It was the way she looked at me with love stamped in her amber eyes, and I couldn't deny I was beginning to feel the same way.

Chapter 7
Quinn

All I'd been doing for over an hour was practicing my jumps then falling on my butt. Frustration rode me hard. If I kept falling, I wouldn't stand a chance at beating Tessa.

I dipped back to what I'd learned when I'd been skating. My warm-up routine had been forward and backward crossovers followed by forward and backward edges then jumps and spins. I hadn't competed long enough to perfect every jump or spin, but I knew the basics. My goal was to get my old routine down pat then add a new jump to the mix. Tessa was probably thinking I didn't have anything new up my sleeve.

With Mozart in my ears, I started my warm-up routine again. The more I skated around the ice, the more the memories of when I'd competed returned. Suddenly, anxiety wormed its way into my stomach, churning and turning.

Breathe. Don't think about when you fell twice in your last competition... or how Tessa laughed at you.

Shaking my wrists, I continued around the ice, breathing deep and pushing the past and Tessa out of my head.

Okay. Just let yourself go.

I turned up the music on my phone, getting lost in Mozart, and went in for a jump, my arms tucked into my chest. As I came out of the jump, my left foot landed at an odd angle, causing pain to ricochet up my leg as I fell on my butt.

No. No. No. Please don't let anything be wrong.

I sat there with my eyes closed, rubbing my ankle as I prayed. I moved my foot around in a circle, one way then the other, wincing as sharp pain crawled up my calf.

Okay, girl. Stand up. Put pressure on it. That will tell you the real story.

I pressed my gloved hands on the ice and slowly pushed myself upright. I bit my lip, willing the pain and throbbing to go away as I skated over to the perimeter of the rink.

Ow. Stupid girl. You shouldn't have made a deal you had no business making.

Once I was leaning against the boards, I wiggled my left foot again. Maybe I could work out the kinks. After another wiggle, I tried to skate around the ice, or at least out to the middle and back just to be sure the pain wasn't all in my head. But as I put pressure on my left foot, I wobbled. Something was wrong.

You've been in this situation before, and it was a minor sprain that didn't interfere with your competition at that time. Ice your ankle and wrap it when you get home. It's probably just bruised.

My hour was almost up anyway, so it was best to call it quits for the moment. I didn't have the ice again until Sunday after church. So I had four days to rest my ankle.

After I managed to get off the ice, I pulled my earbuds out and dropped down on a bench close to the entrance.

"Excuse me." A baritone voice made me flinch. "Are you done for the evening?" A bearded man in a navy-blue uniform with a name tag that read Stewart stood before me.

"Yes, sir. I'll be just a few minutes."

"Give me a shout when you leave," he said. "I'll be in the office right by the entrance." Then he walked away.

I texted Liam to come get me. Then I proceeded to untie my skates when my phone beeped with a reply from Liam.

I've asked Maiken to pick you up. Carter and I are not back from Newton yet. We had to pick up some supplies for Dad. Maiken should be on his way.

My stomach dipped as the door creaked opened. I was expecting to see Maiken not Brianna.

She removed her slouchy knit hat then mussed her bangs with her fingers. "Hi, Stew. Is my dad here?"

Stew fiddled with the keys in his hands. "He left five minutes ago. I'm closing up for the night."

"I won't be long, then," she said. "So, Quinn, how was practice? Are you ready?"

After one practice? Far from it.

I rubbed my sore ankle. "I'm getting there."

She leaned against the backboard that surrounded the rink. "My dad said we could have the rink one week from this Sunday around one."

I counted the days in my head. Eleven wasn't enough to perfect my routine. But if I asked for more time, Tessa would take that to mean I was scared, and she would use my fear to get in my head.

"That should work," I said.

What about your ankle? I hoped it would be fine by then.

"Good." She typed on her phone. "I got the date on the calendar. I'm sending Tessa the date too."

I traded my skates for my boots then packed up. "Can I ask you a question?"

She lowered her phone, giving me her undivided attention.

"Why are you doing all this? I mean why are you so set on seeing Tessa and me get along?" Brianna Masters had never been nice or involved in anything that didn't benefit her. To a certain extent, she and Tessa were alike.

"Honestly, Tessa needs to stop treating people like dirt."

I could feel creases forming on my forehead. Surely Brianna wasn't just coming to that realization. *If she is, why now?*

Her glossy lips split into a smile. "I know what you're thinking. How come I haven't done anything about Tessa before?"

I hiked a shoulder. "Yeah." I didn't know how to tell Brianna that she had been like Tessa as long as I could remember.

Her throat bobbed. "I need Tessa on the squad. We've got a great chance to go to the national cheerleading competition. I can't have her suspended or kicked off the squad."

Ah. Her motives were all her own. And I thought she'd changed from being a snob to a person who wanted to help.

I picked up my phone, which was on the bench next to me.

"Quinn." Brianna's voice was soft. "Did you not like my answer?"

At least she was intuitive and honest. *Pay her the same respect.*

"Your answer was fine." That was the truth. "I'm just wondering why you've decided to do something about the feud between Tessa and me now. You've been head cheerleader for a couple of years."

She sat down next to me. "I'm embarrassed to say I was like Tessa. I was a bully. But since Alex died, I'm trying to be a better person." She let out a sad laugh. "He hated when I was mean to people." She sighed. "I don't want to be like that anymore."

"Alex was an amazing guy," I said softly.

"We had so many plans." She picked at her glove. "Look, I'm going to do what I can to make sure I get through to Tessa. But my advice to you is, the more you stand up to her, the more she'll back down. She preys on the weak. Again, I know because I was like her."

I hadn't run from her since well before her party. So maybe I had changed. And the skate-off was just the thing to show her I wasn't afraid to compete with her as well.

"Even your brother Carter agrees," Brianna said.

I did a double take. Sure, Brianna and Carter were seniors. They knew each other. But I didn't know they talked about me. "Why would you talk to Carter about me?" *And why would my brother talk about me to her?*

She giggled. "I guess you should know, Carter and I have been hanging out as friends." She was quick to add the last word.

Well, one thing was certain—Celia would be happy that Brianna wasn't interested in Liam. I didn't have feelings about Carter and Brianna hanging out or dating for that matter. My brother deserved someone who was nice and caring, and if Brianna had in fact changed, then I was cool with her.

"He told you to help me. Didn't he?" That would explain Brianna's sudden interest in Tessa and me.

"Oh no. Not at all. I was serious in everything I just told you."

Brianna didn't strike me as the type of girl to take orders from anyone. So ninety-nine percent of me believed her. Then again, it didn't matter. What mattered was getting Tessa off my back, and if Brianna wanted to help, I wasn't going to say no.

The entrance door creaked before a cold wind swept in followed by Maiken. As soon as I set eyes on him, my brain turned to goo.

Brianna rose. "We'll talk soon." She said hi to Maiken as she left the rink.

Maiken swaggered in, his hair sticking out that navy-blue knit beanie I loved. "Hey, babe. How was practice?"

I quivered at not only his Southern drawl, but at how he called me babe. "I think I might've sprained my left ankle."

He hurried to kneel in front of me as though he were a doctor. "No way. Let me see."

I giggled. "Okay, doc."

Before I could protest, he took off my boot. "I've sprained my ankle twice in basketball. Wiggle it for me."

I did as he said, hoping my foot didn't stink.

With a light touch, he pressed his fingers all around my ankle. "Does it hurt when I touch it?"

At the moment, I felt no pain. Instead, my heart was beating to a different drum as I concentrated on his magical fingers and the way he smelled of the great outdoors. "No."

He slipped my boot back on and stood, holding out his hand. "Try to walk on it."

Once I was on my feet, I felt a weak twinge of pain, but it wasn't as bad as earlier. "It's okay."

"It might swell tonight," he said. "Keep it elevated as much as you can and put ice on it."

I saluted him. "Yes, doc."

His arm went around my waist while the other swooped around my thighs. "Just in case, I'll carry you to the car."

I busted out laughing. "Are you my knight in shining armor?"

"I'm your prince charming."

He sure was, and as he carried me out and into the cold night air, I knew I could beat Tessa, sprained ankle or not.

Chapter 8

Maiken

The thirteen members of the basketball team were scattered around the locker room, getting ready for practice. Guys chatted about the NFL football playoffs, others dressed, and some texted on their phones.

A thick wall of tension hung in the stinky air, suffocating me. I felt like we were getting ready for some type of war, and all of us were afraid of the outcome. We hadn't practiced in two days, so maybe that was the reason for the somber mood.

We had to come together as a team. We had to show Coach that we were good players and that we could win games. We'd certainly worked together on the Thompson farm the morning prior. But a farm and the basketball court were two different playing fields.

I bent over and tied my basketball shoes. After Coach Dean's speech the other morning about scouts, teamwork, and college, I knew that I would do whatever it took to make the team work, even if that meant biting my tongue on the court when Chase got on my nerves.

As I stood and glanced around at the gloom on everyone's faces, I decided I needed to say something. I felt, as the newbie, that I was the one who was causing all the problems with the team. After all, I was trying to play point guard and not doing a very good job.

I cleared my throat. "Can I have everyone's attention?"

Some of the boys came around from the back side, where more lockers were situated, and the rest stopped what they were doing except for Chase.

No surprise there.

Liam nudged Chase, who was putting on his socks.

"What?" Chase asked. "I don't have to listen to him."

Chase had been one moody SOB since we'd returned from Christmas break. One day, he and I were at each other's throats, and the next, he was clamping his mouth shut and walking away. But if I really thought about when he was nice and when he wasn't, his mood changed when Quinn was around.

Whatever.

I growled so loudly, I swore the lockers shook. "What the fuck is it going to take for you to wise up, Stevens?"

He rose, hands fisted, chest out, ready to take me on.

Liam pushed him down. "Listen for once in your life."

"Or maybe you want to continue to shovel manure," Woods fired back. "No offense, Liam."

Liam raised his hands. "No worries, man."

Chase glanced around, his face red and his eyes narrowed.

Miller, who was beside Chase, slapped him on the back. "Man, look. We're a team. Give Maxwell a chance."

I hopped up on a bench, pinning a look on each player. "I know I don't deserve for you to listen to me. I know I've been just as much of a jerk as Chase has."

Chase made a sound that I ignored as I continued. "I can play this game. However, I am having a rough time with the point guard position only because I was a shooting guard for a long time. But I know this game." I took a breath as some of the players nodded my way. "I'm sorry for my actions during the first home game, and Chase, I'm sorry I hit you." That last part was easier than I'd thought it would be. "What I did was unprofessional and uncalled for." I smoothed a hand over my hair. "I want to win games. I want scouts to look at me. I want them to look at each one of you." I waved my hand around. "But I can't play this game without you. Starting today, we play as a team." I paused at their nods. "Starting today, we leave our differences off the court." They nodded more vigorously. "I promise all of you I will hustle and give everything I have when I'm out on the court. What say you?"

Hoots and hollers zipped around in agreement.

I jumped down and extended my hand to Chase, who was quiet. "Truce, man."

The locker room went completely quiet. A pin drop could be heard.

He gnawed on his lip.

I didn't know if what I'd said resonated with him or not, but it sure made me feel good. I probably sounded like a weirdo, but I was sincere, honest, and I was tired. Something had to give in my life. Something good had to happen, because I'd been feeling all doom and gloom for too long. The only person who'd shined a light in my life that I could honestly say took away the depression I had been feeling was Quinn. All I had to do was set eyes on her, and I felt like the weight of the world wasn't pushing me down.

Chase sighed heavily before he took my hand. "We're never going to be friends, Maxwell. But I do want to win games. I do want scouts to notice me, and I never want to work on the farm again." He grinned as we shook hands.

A rumble of laughter erupted as Chase and I sealed our deal.

As the voices quieted, someone clapped. I turned to find Coach Dean and Kade standing near the entrance that led to the showers.

What's Kade doing here? Maybe Kade was there to talk about my grades. Maybe that was the topic of their conversation yesterday after Kade had dropped me off at school.

Coach swiveled his head at all the players then back at Chase and me. "I'm very pleased at what I heard." If I weren't mistaken, Coach had tears in his brown eyes. "So let's get out there and show me how to play as a team. But first, today is the day we vote for a team captain. The ballots are in the gym. Before you warm up, cast your vote and slip it in the box."

Liam leaned into me. "I think you should be captain."

I didn't make the speech to be captain. Frankly, I'd forgotten that we were even voting that day. I had no desire to be captain, not this year anyway. My life was up in the air with Mom and her sister, and somewhere deep inside my gut, I had a feeling that Ashford wasn't going to be our permanent home. Maybe that was because my mom seemed a little more relaxed in Georgia than in Massachusetts. Plus, she was closer to her sister than my aunt and uncle.

I prodded Kade with my eyes, trying to find out why he was there.

"Oh, and one more thing," Coach said. "I want to introduce you to Kade Maxwell. He's going to be my assistant for the near future."

"Are you going somewhere, Coach?" one of the freshmen asked.

Coach slipped his hands into his pants pockets. "You're going to find out soon enough, but my wife just found out that she has to have major surgery. It's a procedure that will keep her off her feet for a few weeks. I'm going to try to be at games, but family comes first. So Kade will be filling in. The floor is yours, Kade."

Kade, who was slightly taller than us six-footers, nodded. "I played basketball in my freshman year. So my knowledge of the game is a little rusty. I'm going to rely on all of you to help me with plays." He swung his copper gaze around the room. "My expectations are simple and align with Coach Dean's. No mouthing off. No fighting." He nailed Chase and me with a stern look. "And above all else, I want to see respect for each other, respect for Coach and me, and respect for the game."

Ten seconds passed before Coach clapped his hands again. "Get out there."

The team scattered, buzzing with excitement as lockers opened and slammed shut before the room began to empty.

I started for the door when Coach snagged me. "Maxwell, can I have a word?"

Chase and Liam, who were just about to walk out, hesitated.

"Go," I said. "I'll be right there." I had an idea what was about to take place or what Coach was about to say. I hadn't had a chance to talk to him about my grades because practice had been canceled for the last two days and he'd left school early the day before.

Nevertheless, when the door clicked shut, leaving Kade, Coach, and me alone, I held my breath. I'd just given the speech of the century, asking my team to give me a chance, telling them I would hustle and give everything I had when I was out on the court. Yet I couldn't give anything if I was benched.

My heartbeat punched my ribs. "I'm sorry, Coach. I was going to tell you."

Coach tilted his head. "Tell me what?"

My gaze jerked to Kade's. He shrugged. Coach didn't know.

Well, I was on a roll with apologizing and telling the truth, so I might as well get it over with. I inhaled deeply. "I'm failing chemistry and English." As I delivered the news, I cringed.

Coach removed his ball cap, scratched his balding head, then replaced the hat. Disappointment washed over him more than anger, which was more of a jab to the gut. He was counting on me, and I'd just ruined everything. My speech certainly didn't mean anything now.

"I promise I will get my grades up," I was quick to add.

"I've already laid down the law with him," Kade said to Coach. "But I know school policy dictates that he can't play."

Coached paced. "I was going to tell you I lifted your suspension, but now you've put me in a difficult situation."

"I don't want you to give me any special treatment," I said. I didn't. That wouldn't be right for me or anyone else.

"School policy says that students don't flunk more than one major subject in order to play sports." He kept pacing. "So that means you need to bring up your grade in one or the other before you can play."

I was on the borderline in chemistry with an overall grade of sixty-four. "If I pass my chemistry test next Tuesday, that should put me over the top."

Coach stopped pacing, and his lips flattened into a thin line. "Then you better pass that test. However, you'll sit out Monday's game. That will fulfill your suspension."

I puffed out my cheeks. "Thank you."

"Get out of here," Coach ordered in a tone that had me moving my feet.

When I grabbed the door handle, I asked, "Coach, don't you get our grades?"

"I do, but with my wife's medical issue, I haven't looked at them." Then Coach started talking to Kade.

My phone rang when I was out in the hall. I snatched it out of the pocket of my sweatshirt. "Hey, Mom."

She sniffled. "Are you at a place you can talk?"

"Yeah," I barely said, knowing that her next words would change everything.

Chapter 9

Maiken

Flames flickered in the fireplace, keeping my attention on the roaring fire while I waited for Mom to call back. Every now and then, I diverted my gaze to my phone, which sat ominously on the square, glass-topped coffee table as though it were a bomb ready to go off. But no one was moving to get out of the room. I certainly couldn't move. The word *cancer* had a way of niggling in and making me feel numb and frozen.

"She said nine p.m. Right?" Kade asked from the oversized chair adjacent to the couch on which Lacey and I were sitting.

"Yeah," I said as I continued to stare at the dancing flames across from me.

"You did well at practice today," Kade said.

I knew he was trying to take my mind off my mom. But it wasn't working. Sure, practice had been great—at least Coach had been stoked about how well we'd played. I wasn't sure how I'd even bounced a ball considering the news Mom had given me.

Lacey scooted closer and rested a hand on my shoulder. "Maiken, the medical community has come a long way with treating breast cancer. Did your mom say what stage your aunt is in?"

"She said she would tell us everything tonight."

Kade leaned forward and rested his elbows on his knees. "We're here for you and your family, Maiken."

My dad's moral code had always been "family above all else," and my uncle and cousins weren't any different. I knew my mom lived by the same code, but her side of the family wasn't as big or strong as the Maxwells. My aunt Denise was Mom's only sister, and their parents had died many years ago, which was one of the reasons we'd moved here. She had wanted us boys to have more structure as we grew into men. She felt that Kade, Uncle Martin, and his other sons might afford us that fatherly structure.

At the moment, I didn't need fatherly structure. I needed to be with my mom. "My mom needs me," I mumbled, hopping up. "I'm going to pack."

"Maiken," Kade said. "Let's talk to your mom first. She said she would call at nine. It's about that time."

No matter what my mom had to say, I was leaving as soon as I could. I held my left arm tightly as I crossed the room to stand in front of the fire. Maybe the heat would thaw out my nerves, which felt frozen. Or maybe a run later that night would do me some good. It had been months since I'd last strapped on my running shoes.

My phone rang then vibrated, bouncing on the table. I rushed to answer it then tapped the speaker button. "Mom."

"Are Kade and Lacey there?" she asked.

Lacey scooted to the edge of the couch cushion. "We're all here, Christine."

Kade dragged the wingback chair closer to the phone. I knelt down, taking in as much oxygen as I could.

"So, Maiken told you my sister has breast cancer. Well, what I didn't mention, because I wanted to wait until I had all of you together, is Denise has stage-four breast cancer with a very low prognosis of beating it."

Tears streamed down Lacey's cheeks, and Kade grasped her hand.

I couldn't hold back anymore. I'd done a great job at practice of keeping my emotions bottled up tightly, although if Mom had told me Aunt Denise's prognosis, I probably would've broken down.

Kade lowered his gaze to the carpet. "What are the next steps, Christine?" His tone was somber.

"Honestly, I don't know. Denise needs to makes some decisions on whether she'll have surgery or not. The cancer has spread to her lymph nodes. The doctors want to try chemo first to see if they can get a hold on it before removing her breasts. But stage four might be hard to beat."

"Mom," I choked out. "I want to get on a plane as soon as possible."

"No, Maiken." Her voice was soft and nasally. "I want you to stay with Kade and Lacey. You have school and basketball, and you need to get those grades up."

"You need help with the kids," I protested.

Lacey flashed her green eyes at her husband. "Christine, would you consider sending the kids back here? I'm not working. Baseball season doesn't start for another two months."

Kade kissed the back of Lacey's hand. "We'll get them settled back at my parents' house and get them to school every day."

My mom started crying, and I wanted to jump through the phone and hug her. I also wanted to leap over the table and hug Kade and Lacey.

Lacey sniffled. "You're going to need the free time to focus on your sister."

My mom blew her nose, at least that was how it sounded. "I can't put that burden on you newlyweds. I have eight kids."

Kade chuckled. "It will give us practice. Right, baby?" His

expression toward his wife was dripping with love—a love so strong and deep that I was sure he would die for Lacey.

I wanted that feeling with a girl one day. I wanted to get married and have kids. Like my parents, I wanted lots of children running around. I wanted a big house with lots of land so we could have dogs and cats and, dare I say, farm animals. Maybe Quinn was rubbing off on me.

I cried with Lacey and Mom. Even Kade was shedding tears. I felt helpless, sad, and hurt that our family had to deal with another tragedy.

"Kade." Mom's voice cracked. "I can't... I—"

"Christine, you're our family," Lacey said. "We would do anything, I mean anything, for family. So we don't want to hear another word. The kids will stay with us."

Kade kissed the back of Lacey's hand again. I wanted to hug the heck out of her and Kade.

Mom sighed then shuddered. "Let's talk tomorrow afternoon. Denise has a doctor's appointment, and I need to break the news to the children. Then we can talk particulars. The kids do need to return to school before I need a doctor's note for each of them."

"Sounds good," Kade said.

All of my siblings loved and adored Aunt Denise. I knew that was going to be a tough conversation for my mom. I should've been there to help shoulder their pain.

"Mom, I should be there when you tell everyone."

"Maiken," Mom said. "There'll be plenty of time to console each other. As hard as it might be, please concentrate on school. Promise me."

I would do anything for her. "Of course, Mom."

"I have to run. And Kade and Lacey, I owe you so much. Maiken, I love you dearly." Then the call ended.

The three of us sat there, gaping at the phone. When the fire crackled, I flinched, rose to my feet, and threw my arms around Lacey.

She rubbed a hand up and down by back. "We're here for you." Then she eased away, flattening her soft, small hands on my cheeks. "You hear me? Any time you want to talk, you come to me or Kade."

With so much emotion clogging my throat, all I could do was nod.

"I know how hard it is to lose loved ones," she said softly. "Don't hold back on your feelings. Talk to me or someone. Or what helps me is writing in my journal. Find an outlet that will allow you to express your feelings." Then she pulled me to her. "You're not alone, Maiken."

At times, I felt like I was. I felt as though I'd lost one of my best friends in my dad. He'd always been my hero. But what hurt the most was seeing Mom in pain.

Lacey let go of me, tears sliding down her cheeks. "Excuse me." She darted out of the room.

Confusion had me knitting my brows.

"She's remembering her sister and mom," Kade whispered.

I knew they'd died in a home invasion, but I didn't know the particulars, which didn't matter. What did matter was that Lacey was a strong woman like my mom. From that, I took comfort in knowing that my mom would get through this.

Kade scraped a hand over his jaw. "If you need to stay home from school tomorrow, you can."

I needed something to keep my mind occupied, and school and basketball were the perfect distractions. Or on second thought, maybe they weren't. The way I was feeling might cause me to lash out at Chase. Then the truce we were fostering would go down the tubes.

However, I did want to see Quinn. I wanted to hear her spit out a random fact. I wanted her to give me that shy and flirty smile—the one that was reserved only for me, the one that said she was so glad we'd met and so happy we were boyfriend and girlfriend. Above all else, I just wanted to hug my girl.

Chapter 10

Quinn

I looked for Maiken that Friday morning at school. I looked for him at lunch in the cafeteria. I texted and called him, but I'd gotten no response. A ball of craziness clouded my mind all day. Classes crawled by. Teacher's voices droned like the crickets on a warm summer night. I could count on one hand how many times I hadn't paid attention in classes, and that day made two. The last time was when my granddaddy had died.

I had Liam call Maiken during lunch, and he struck out too.

Maybe Maiken had come down with the flu. He'd been in good spirits and hadn't looked sick when he'd picked me up from the rink two nights ago. Sadly, I hadn't seen him the previous day except briefly in the hall before the first bell had rung. After school, Momma and I had gone to see Granny. I hadn't seen her in a while, and I'd wanted to ask her if I could bring Maiken and Tessa by on Saturday during her monthly poker game. That was the day Tessa and Maiken were teamed up to sell those discount cards for the fundraiser.

I gnawed on a nail as I headed over to the sports complex. My ankle was a smidge better, thanks to Maiken. For the last two days and nights, I'd taken his advice and iced and elevated my ankle every chance I had.

I peeked through the window in the gym. The boys were running up and down the court, but Maiken was nowhere to be found. I saw Coach on the sidelines, but I didn't see Kade. Liam had told me that Kade was now the assistant basketball coach. Surely Kade would be there unless he was sick too.

I wrapped my fingers around the handle of the door when a text beeped on my phone.

Maiken's name brightened my screen and my heart. *Finally.*

Maiken: *Sorry. I've slept most of the day. Long story, but can you come over?*

My fingers got ahead of my brain as I typed, *I'll see you soon.*

I didn't have a car. I didn't even have my license yet. I was sixteen, but I'd put off getting my license until the spring. I wasn't in a rush to drive. Not only that, but even if I had my driver's license, I wouldn't have a car. Momma and Daddy didn't have the money to buy me one. They didn't even have the money to buy Carter and Liam one. Carter had gotten Daddy's old beat-up truck that he'd had for years. And Granny had given Liam Granddaddy's truck after he'd passed.

Celia had a car, though. Then I remembered she had something to do for the school newspaper. I guess I would have to wait until basketball practice was over. Or I could walk. Kade and Lacey were living in a house close to downtown, which wasn't far from school.

I sent Liam a text to let him know where I was and told him to pick me up when he was done. In my haste to get out of the sports complex, it dawned on me that I'd forgotten to ask for the address. So I sent Maiken a text as I made the trek toward downtown.

He responded quickly, and within thirty minutes, I was knocking on the door of the modest two-story brick home. It had three dormers, a deep front porch framing the length of the house, and a two-car attached garage.

The trees rustled in the yard as I waited for someone to answer. After a long minute, I rang the doorbell. Maybe I had the wrong address. Before I could double-check, the lock clicked and the green door swung open.

Maiken gave me a half smile as he peeked out toward the driveway. "Did someone drop you off?"

I stepped in. "I walked from school."

"What about your ankle?"

"Fine." But as I said the word, I felt a dull throbbing in my ankle.

He closed the door. "You should've told me. I would've picked you up. I assumed Liam would be with you. Oh, that's right. He's at basketball practice."

I followed him down a narrow hall until we came to a spacious open room that spilled into the kitchen, where bright lights sprayed down from the ceiling and a spicy scent floated in the air.

I shrugged out of my winter gear. "Is Kade here? He wasn't at practice either."

Maiken took my coat and set it on the wingback chair near the couch. "He's been making arrangements for me."

"Arrangements?" My first thought was macabre and stupid since Maiken was standing before me. My second thought was that he was leaving, and all of a sudden, my belly spun out of control.

Maiken held out his hand. "Let's sit over here."

The sectional couch was inviting, but my legs were locked as I stood in front of the crackling fire.

Footsteps padded in the hall before Lacey entered the family room. As always, she looked beautiful as ever. Her hair was twisted up on her head, and her green eyes sparkled, although I wasn't sure sparkle was the right word because when she glanced at Maiken, that spark went out. "Hi, Quinn. I'm making stew if you would like to stay for dinner."

I nodded. "I'll have to check with my mom."

She crossed the room into the kitchen and turned off the stove. "I'll be in the office, Maiken. Kade is almost done. We should be ready to eat soon."

Once we were alone, Maiken closed his warm hands around my cold ones as he guided me to the couch. I eased down while he sat on the edge of the glass coffee table until our knees touched, or rather my knees were up against his shins.

"You're going to tell me something bad. Aren't you?" My voice wasn't my own.

"I'm going back to…"

I lowered my head, worrying my bottom lip.

He captured my face in his hands. "Hey, babe. Look at me."

The word babe made me blink up at him.

He puffed out his cheeks. "My aunt Denise has stage-four breast cancer." Pain etched his handsome features.

All of a sudden, I couldn't control my emotions. Tears filled my eyes and spilled down my cheeks like a waterfall after a hard rain.

With the tips of his fingers, he swiped across my cheeks, one side then the other. "I'm leaving tomorrow for Georgia."

I cried a little more for his aunt, for him, and for us. I shouldn't have been selfish, but I couldn't help but think he wasn't coming back. "I'm sorry a-about your a-aunt."

You need to be strong for him. He's been through his dad's death, and now his aunt is sick. I wanted to be strong, yet I felt like I was losing him.

As if he were in my head, he said softly, "I'm going to finish the school year here."

I gave him a weak smile, my hands trembling. I should've been relieved, but I was far from it. He might not be living there next year, and that scared me, saddened me, and made me want to bawl my eyes out.

"Kade and I are flying down, and then we'll be driving back with my sisters and brothers so they too can finish out the school year."

Show him that you can be there for him.

I mustered up courage from somewhere deep inside me. "Can I do anything for you?"

He pressed his forehead to mine. "Just being here is helping me so damn much."

I threw my arms around him, holding back more tears. "I'm always here for you."

His hands landed in my hair as he shuddered. "Tell me a random fact." His breath tickled my ear.

I giggled, the act refreshing. "Hugging increases serotonin and makes us feel happy."

"Then never stop hugging me," he said.

I didn't plan on it. I would hug him, kiss him, and make his world as bright as I could.

Chapter 11

Maiken

The guys were shooting baskets when I sauntered into the gym on that Monday afternoon with Kade and the twins, Emma and Ethan.

Kade and I had flown down to Georgia early on Saturday morning, and then we'd driven all day on Sunday, taking turns at the wheel of the family's Suburban. I would've liked to have stayed longer with my mom, but she'd insisted that we return so everyone could get back to school.

Saying goodbye to her was one of the hardest things I'd had to do. I hated to leave her alone to deal with everything that was about to happen with Aunt Denise.

"Maiken, I need you to help Kade and Lacey as much as you can with your brothers and sisters. I'll be fine. I'll call every night," she'd said.

With her pale complexion and the hopelessness that swam in her eyes, I doubted that she would be okay. Yet I would do my part or anything else she asked me to do.

Emma practically skipped into the gym. "I missed school. Is there a game tonight?"

The banners above read Beat Lancaster Christian.

"Yeah, but I'm benched for this game," I said to my fifteen-year-old sister, not that she was even listening to me. She spotted her friend Dana in the stands and headed in that direction.

Kade strutted over to Coach Dean. He was stoked to be coaching. In fact, he didn't want to miss the game that night, which was another reason we'd driven back as soon as we could.

Ethan had been quiet since leaving Mom in Georgia. He was about to follow Emma when I clutched his arm. "Dude, what's wrong?" I'd tried to talk to him earlier, but he'd shrugged me off.

He hunched his shoulders, his brown hair falling forward as he cast his gaze downward. "When are our lives going to be normal? First Dad, now Aunt Denise. Mom looks awful. She's been crying every night."

I was glad Mom had sent me back to Ashford without her, only because I knew that if I'd stayed, I would have been feeling down in the dumps like Ethan, especially if I were listening to Mom cry every night.

I guided him away from everyone to a spot at the end of the bleachers where no one was around. "Listen to me. It's killing me that Mom is in pain, that Aunt Denise may not have long to live. Hell, the pain from Dad's death hasn't gone away. But as the oldests, you and me and even Emma have to step up and be there for our family."

"I get that. I've been trying. But we can't keep moving. We can't keep leaving friends behind. Mom has been talking about staying in Georgia permanently. I want a girlfriend that I don't have to say goodbye to at the end of the school year."

That last line gave me whiplash. "I know. Me too." I had no words of wisdom or comfort for him. The thought of leaving Quinn felt like a crushing force of pain that gripped my chest like someone had dropped a boulder on me.

Ethan flicked his hair off his forehead. It had turned a lighter shade of brown from the sun in Georgia. "Are you ready to leave Quinn?"

Swallowing what felt like razors, I whispered, "No."

"You're in love with her. Aren't you?" Ethan's tone was mournful.

I hiked a shoulder. "I don't know." I knew I didn't want to leave her. I knew that she made me feel things that were new and exciting and downright scary at times—in a good way, though. "What I do know, bro—family comes first." If Mom wanted to settle down in Georgia, then that was what we would do.

He nodded as Liam jogged over to us, dressed in sweats. Actually, the team was all dressed in black Kensington High sweatpants and royal-blue hoodies, which were part of the team's wardrobe.

"Ethan," Liam said. "Good to see you."

Barely smiling, Ethan scaled the bleachers to sit beside Emma.

Liam stabbed a finger at Ethan. "What's wrong with him?"

Life. "Family thing. He'll be fine." At least I hoped he would be. I wasn't sure I would be, but at that moment, I couldn't think about what the future held for Ethan or any of us.

Dad would always sit us down just before a move to another military base and say, "I know this is hard on all of you, but I want you to make the best of your new home." That included school and friends.

"So Tessa's been waiting for you. She is pissed that you missed the fundraiser on Saturday."

I rolled my eyes. In a way, I'd been looking forward to selling those discount cards only because Quinn had had a great idea in selling most of them to her grandmother and friends.

I eyed the cheerleaders in the distance. "Did she sell any cards?"

Tessa waved.

"Not one. She didn't even try according to Brianna, who, by the way, is pissed. But Tessa promised her she would sell all of them when you returned."

I wasn't a magic salesman, although maybe Quinn's offer to sell to her grandmother was still open.

"Brianna and I sold all but two," Liam bragged. "Actually, most of the other teams did as well." He hit me on the arm. "So you need to get hot now that you're back. Do your part for the team."

"Quinn said your grandmother would buy," I said.

"About that… Since you weren't here, Quinn told us to hit up my granny. Anyway, have you talked to my sister?" The concerned inflection in his tone made me zero in on him.

"We've swapped texts all weekend, but nothing since yesterday morning before I left Georgia. Why? What's wrong?"

"Last night, the ankle she bruised while skating the other day—well, she twisted it again."

"Sprained?" While a sprain wasn't good, I crossed my fingers that she hadn't broken it.

He nodded his head of shaggy, brown hair. "Yep. She hopped down off the box she uses to stand on to brush Apple, and her ankle gave out. She's on crutches."

Yikes. "Is she going to be able to skate?" I knew she could beat Tessa, but not with a bad ankle.

"Not sure. I got to get back, and Coach wants to talk to you, by the way." He loped back to the team.

I ambled over to Coach and Kade. "Hey, Coach. Who's playing point guard tonight?" Since I wasn't, I was curious who was.

With his focus on the team, he said, "I'm shifting things around a bit. I'm going to see how Chase does in that position."

I cocked an eyebrow, wondering if I'd heard him correctly.

Coach blew his whistle. "Everyone, on the bench."

Everyone shuffled off, most welcoming me back. Of course, Chase didn't say anything to me.

I started to sit with the team on the bleachers, but Coach stopped me. "Stay where you are."

Okay. I looked at Liam for answers. He shrugged with a cheeky grin that said he knew something I didn't.

Coach snagged his clipboard off the bench. "Lancaster Christian is going to be tough to beat tonight. So I want all of you giving a hundred and ten percent. Now, Kade will be lead since I won't be here, and Maiken will assist Kade if need be."

I reared back.

"Woods, as we discussed earlier, you'll move to shooting guard."

I stared at Chase, who, for the first time since I'd met him, wasn't wearing his emotions on his sleeve. His pimpled face was completely blank.

"Chase," Coach continued, "you'll be point guard, which means passing the ball and reading the plays. Malone"—he pointed at a lanky freshman beside Chase—"you'll take on power forward. Liam, you're still center, and Miller, small forward. I expect each of you to listen to Kade. We need to start winning more games. Teamwork. Passing. Scoring. Are we clear?"

"Yes, Coach," the team said in unison.

"Good. Now, Chase, do you want to share the news with Maiken?" It was more of a statement than a question.

Chase jutted out his chin. "You're the new captain."

My jaw hit the floor. "Come again?"

Liam repeated the words in more of an excited tone. "You're the new captain, dude."

How is that possible? Did Coach pick me? He'd said he had the final say. Regardless, I was the new kid. I was also the one who didn't deserve the role. I had poor grades, I wasn't playing well, and I'd displayed unsportsmanlike conduct.

"We had one vote for Liam and twelve votes for you," Coach added.

I studied Chase. "You voted for me?" I'd been the one who wrote Liam's name on the ballot.

His shoulders almost touched his ears. "Maybe."

It was obvious to me he didn't want to announce it to all the guys when in fact Coach had.

Kade cleared his throat. "Maiken, it doesn't matter. What matters is you have an opportunity to bring this team together and lead."

"Dude," Miller piped in, "your speech was off the charts. All of us talked earlier. We want you as our captain. Isn't that right, Chase?"

Chase sighed. "All right. I admit, Maxwell, that you did light a fire under my ass. I'm in for giving you a chance. But that doesn't mean you get to tell me what position I'm playing."

"He's not going to do that," Coach said. "But I expect both of you"—he wagged his finger between Chase and me—"to work together, which means no fighting, and that includes yelling or punching each other. Are we all in agreement?" His gaze circled the team.

Nods and yeses zipped around.

"Very well, then. I need a word with Maiken alone. Kade, take over from here."

Kade grabbed Coach's clipboard as Coach guided me out of the gym and into the hall. We settled near the glass case where trophies were displayed for championship wins in football, hockey, baseball, and basketball.

Coach opened his stance and folded his arms over his chest. His dark eyes narrowed. "I expect you to pass your chemistry test tomorrow if you want to play Wednesday. However, going forward as captain, you need to set an example, which means outside of school policy, I expect you to maintain a C or higher in all your classes and lead this team, which means perfect behavior on and off the court. Can you do all that?"

I was still trying to wrap my mind around Chase voting for me. "Yes, sir."

"Alex Baker was a great captain, and I see a lot of him in you. You have the rest of this season and your junior and senior years to really do something great with this team, son." He poked my chest just above my heart. "Believe in yourself. Believe in others. Put your heart into the game you love. If you do that, your skills will shine brightly enough for scouts to take an interest in you."

All I could do was smile even though deep down, I was afraid I might not be there next year or the year after. But that was a worry for another day. Right then, I would do all I could to make Coach proud of me, to make the team shine, and to play like I'd never played before.

Chapter 12

Quinn

Momma sang softly to a Frank Sinatra song as she drove me to Shakers. I couldn't help but sing along with her to a classic, "My Way."

Momma had a pretty voice, but I couldn't carry a tune. Still, it was fun to belt out a song together in the car. On occasion, she would listen to my type of music like 5 Seconds of Summer.

She bounced over a bump, and the car jarred me forward, causing my phone to topple to my lap.

"The town needs to fix those potholes," she complained, more to herself than me. Then she lowered the radio. "I don't want you out too late. You need to rest your ankle."

Luck wasn't on my side. My sore ankle, which I thought I'd originally sprained while practicing at the rink, was now officially wrapped in a bandage and swollen. The night before when I'd been brushing Apple, I'd missed one of the steps on the two-step box I used and twisted my ankle.

The universe was definitely giving me a sign. It was saying, "Don't skate against Tessa because you won't win." I probably wouldn't if my ankle didn't at least heal a little by Sunday. I'd skated on a sore ankle before, but not a sprained one, and I didn't think six days was long enough for the swelling to go down, particularly if I kept walking on it.

Nevertheless, I was bummed. I'd had a second practice session the day before at the rink. My jumps were good, but not perfect yet. My spins were on point, and I'd felt like I could conquer anything.

Momma kept her eyes on the road. "Are you canceling the competition?"

I gave her a sidelong glance. Her small gold loop earring shimmered from the lights of an oncoming car in the other lane. "I'll talk to Brianna." I suspected it would be hard to change the date. It wasn't like the rink was free anytime, especially this time of year when hockey games galore were scheduled.

The large neon sign for Shakers twinkled in the distance as we approached the new hamburger place on the outskirts of downtown Ashford.

Maiken had texted me to meet him there. The team had won against Lancaster Christian, so most of the guys wanted to celebrate. I was sure I would see the cheerleaders, which meant Tessa would be there too.

Momma slowly navigated the parking lot, which had cars parked four rows deep. "Wow, busy place tonight."

For a Monday, I would agree. Then again, the restaurant was new and a prime hangout spot for the high school kids.

She pulled up to the main entrance. "Do you need help?"

"No, ma'am. I got this." *Maybe.* I was using crutches on the doctor's orders, but maneuvering out of the passenger seat before I could stand up on crutches would be a challenge.

Taking a deep breath, I climbed out and set both feet on the concrete.

Here goes nothing.

I used the door as my anchor to push me upright. When I did, I swallowed down the pain. Yep, I wouldn't be able to skate anytime soon. I hobbled on my right foot as I clumsily grabbed the crutches.

Just as I did, large hands came into view from behind me. I was hoping it was Maiken, but when I tossed a look over my shoulder, I found Chase.

He snatched the crutches out of the car. "Let me help you."

"Thank you, Chase," Momma said. "You're a peach."

I giggled for nothing more than to forget the throbbing in my ankle, although the words peach and Chase didn't exactly go together. He was a gentleman, nonetheless, helping me get situated with my crutches.

"I got her, Mrs. Thompson. She's in good hands."

Momma regarded me for some sign that I agreed.

"I'll get a ride home with Liam," I said before hobbling away so Chase could close the car door.

Once the taillights on Momma's car faded, I began my trek into the restaurant.

"Surely you're not going to compete with that injury," Chase said as he stayed by my side, seemingly afraid I would fall at any minute.

I might just face-plant before I even got to the entrance because of the awkwardness of using crutches. "Not sure."

"I'm rooting for you, Quinn." His tone was sweet and believable.

Stopping, I leaned on my crutches. "Why? She's your sister." If I were in his shoes, I would cheer for my own blood despite how I felt. Or at least I wouldn't brag that I wanted my sibling's enemy to win.

His dark eyes searched my face. "She also needs to stop bullying you."

"And you think skating is going to do the trick?" Brianna thought so. But I was curious what Chase thought.

He harrumphed. "I don't. Whether you win or lose, Tessa will always be Tessa."

"She made a deal," I mumbled as if trying to convince myself that Tessa wouldn't break our deal.

He feathered his fingers through his unruly brown hair. "Deals can be broken."

My underarms were beginning to hurt. "Do you have a better idea?"

He smirked as if he had the perfect plan. "I know my sister. She will pounce on anyone who fears her. So show her you're not afraid of her. The more you stand up to her, the more she'll move on to someone else or something else."

That settled it. I couldn't back out despite my injury.

I inched closer to the entrance. "Do you thrive on fear?" I had to ask since he had his own feud with Maiken, although neither of them backed down from one another.

"You mean with Maxwell?"

One of the glass doors opened, and Maiken strutted out. His features were tight, hard, and wary. "What's going on?"

Chase lifted his chin. "Just having a friendly conversation."

A muscle jumped in Maiken's jaw. "Is that so? You're not trying to move in on my girl?"

Chase rolled his eyes. "If I wanted to, I would have already. Nice chatting, Quinn. Remember what I said." Then he brushed past Maiken, bumping his shoulder.

When Chase was gone, Maiken's attitude shifted from macho jealousy to tender and caring. "Should I carry you?"

I shied away. "Not this time." Although if I weren't walking into a room full of kids whom I suspected had their phones primed to take pictures, I would've done all I could to jump into Maiken's arms.

Maiken held open the door. "What were you and Chase talking about?"

I felt special that two boys liked me, but I didn't like all the tension and fighting when they were in the same space together. I wanted everyone to get along. I wanted everyone to be nice to one another. But I knew that was an impossible feat when emotions were involved, not to mention raging hormones, which were partially responsible for driving our actions. I'd overheard Daddy saying that to Momma the other night.

"His sister," I said as the warm air from inside breezed over me.

The restaurant was buzzing with loud voices and the clanking of dishes and silverware. I was surprised anyone could hear anything.

Maiken rested a hand on my lower back. "We're at the booth in the corner."

I was hopping around tables when, lo and behold, Tessa jumped up from a chair. She had a smirk the size of Rhode Island on her face. "I guess you can't compete." Her inky-black eyes were full of happiness. "That means I win."

Anger, hot and sticky, made me glare hard at my enemy. "Who says I can't compete?"

She tipped her head to the side, all smug and witchy. "You're going to skate in six days?"

The people at the tables in the near vicinity ceased all conversation.

No time like the present to take Chase's advice. But as I opened my mouth, I couldn't think of a comeback. "Sit down, Tessa." My tone was firm.

She puffed out her cheeks. "So are you forfeiting? You know if you do, I win."

A vision of me butting her head with mine flashed before me. Maybe if I did something like that, I would knock some niceness into her. A girl could dream.

"Don't worry. I'll be ready." *Liar.*

She studied me, not knowing if I was serious or telling a fib. Either way, the disgusting look she was giving me made me want to poke her with one of my crutches.

I had a good mind to do just that because she was blocking my path to the booth, and I needed to sit down. My underarms were on fire, my ankle throbbed to no end, and I was hungrier than a bear coming out of hibernation.

She sighed, sliding out of my way as if to say she would let me pass just this once.

The people around us started up their conversations again, but I tuned them out. In fact, I didn't even notice who Tessa was sitting with or who from school was watching. Maybe because as I passed her, she said Maiken's name.

I slowly turned around to find Tessa's hand on Maiken's chest. My anger morphed into a raging river of fury. I definitely understood Maiken's jealousy over Chase, but I wasn't about to walk away like Chase had.

"We're still on for tomorrow after school?" she asked Maiken in a flirtatious yet bragging tone, most likely because she knew I was listening.

The tables on the other side of the restaurant probably heard her too since her voice had been elevated to make sure I didn't miss a word.

Stars coated my vision. The greasy odor that permeated the air turned rancid. I refused to believe the worst, but my mind couldn't dismiss the thoughts I was having. I'd missed the basketball game, and the world seemed to have shifted on its axis.

Maiken set his big blue eyes on me as though he were pleading with me, or maybe he was trying to tell me he was sorry. "I'll be there."

My anger turned to fury as a deep, throaty noise erupted from me.

Tessa let out a cold-hearted laugh as she pivoted on her two-inch-heeled boots. "I told you that night at my party, you haven't won anything."

Don't cry. Don't you dare shed a tear. If you do, she's won. Then Chase's words rang in my ears. "The more you challenge her, the more she'll move onto someone else."

As I stood before my enemy, I knew she wouldn't back down, not when it came to Maiken. She'd wanted him even before she knew I liked him, way before he and I had started dating. In some respects, I couldn't blame her for trying to get the boy. After all, Maiken was every girl's dream—tall, sandy-blond hair, blue eyes, and muscles in all the right places.

Not only that, whatever I said next wouldn't matter. My words wouldn't change her belief that she'd won. Actions might, though. So despite how mad I was, I waltzed up to my boyfriend, gave him a huge smile, and tugged on his shirt as best I could on crutches. My intentions were to kiss him and drive my message home to Tessa that she hadn't won anything.

Yet when I craned my neck upward, he shook his head ever so slightly. Then he wrapped his arm around my shoulders and tried to guide me to the booth.

I hated to look around. I hated to see all the expressions on people's faces. The good news was the chatter had started up again, taking the attention away from Tessa and me. The bad news—I felt small, embarrassed, and seethed with so much anger that I wanted to explode. And at the moment, my anger was directed at Maiken.

Suddenly, I didn't want to be there with him or around anyone.

"I need to use the restroom," I said in a low voice to Maiken. "I'll be back." I retraced my steps until I was standing at the hostess podium. I didn't need to use the bathroom. I needed a moment alone to collect my emotions.

The sign for the restroom hung overhead. I started in that direction when Chase came out of the men's room.

He cocked his head. "What's wrong? You look pissed."

That was an understatement.

"My sister?"

And Maiken.

I shrugged.

"Want to get out of here?" he asked.

"Can you take me home?" The words flew out without me thinking.

He beamed as though he'd won the grand prize. "Come on."

I all but ran out of Shakers, inhaling the fresh, clean winter air as tears burned their way to the surface.

"Wait here," Chase said. "I'll get my car."

I leaned on my crutches as he jogged off and out of sight. I'd barely taken in my next breath when Maiken came out.

"What are you doing?" he asked. "I thought you needed to use the bathroom."

"Really? Why did you n-not want to k-kiss me in there? And what is going on between y-you and Tessa?" I was shivering rather than stuttering.

Celia buttoned up her coat as she came out of Shakers. "Quinn, are you okay?"

No. No. No.

"Celia," Maiken said. "Can you leave us alone?"

She raised her hands. "I just want to check on my friend."

"I'm fine, Celia," I said.

She huffed as she rolled her eyes. "Right. We'll talk tomorrow." She hurried back in.

"I haven't seen you since I got back from Georgia, and you

weren't at the game tonight. So how could I tell you about Tessa? She wants to sell those discount cards tomorrow for the fundraiser."

I'd forgotten all about that. Liam and Brianna had sold most of theirs to Granny and her friends, so I couldn't use that angle anymore.

"As far as kissing you…" He inched closer to me. "I want to so badly. Hell, that's all I thought about on the drive up from Georgia. But you only wanted to kiss me to show Tessa something. That's not a reason to kiss me."

Chase drove up.

Maiken looked at him then at me. "You're leaving with him?" He sounded so hurt.

"He's just giving me a ride home," I said, feeling like I was the biggest harridan on the planet.

Maiken mashed his lips into a thin line and studied me for a brief second that felt like hours as the pain oozed off him and onto me. Then he slowly backed away.

"M-Maiken," I said.

He raised his hands, shook his head, and walked away.

I couldn't help but cry. In that moment, I hated feeling like I couldn't control my emotions. I hated feeling like the world was crashing down around me.

Why is liking a boy so hard?

Chapter 13

Maiken

The rink was teeming with people hooting and hollering at the men's hockey game. I'd had the worst day possible with the exception of one. My chemistry teacher had gone out of his way to grade my test that day after school, and I'd passed with a seventy, thus making my overall average a passing grade in the class, which meant I could play in tomorrow's night game.

Aside from that, my stomach was a wad of knots. One moment, I was angry with Quinn, and the next, I was kicking myself in the butt for walking away.

It had taken all I had not to devour her lips and kiss her until someone had to call the paramedics. But she didn't need to use me to get to Tessa, especially not in front of a burger joint full of high school kids who'd probably had their phones ready to snap pictures.

I'd run out to talk to her, but when Chase had pulled up, I'd lost all train of thought. Or rather my only thought had been to start a fight with Chase. That wouldn't have accomplished anything. Besides, he hadn't forced her to get into his car.

Surprisingly, he'd gone out of his way at basketball practice earlier to let me know he'd taken Quinn straight home last night and nothing more. I would've decked him if he had tried something.

He was becoming a walking contradiction as of late. When I'd found him walking into Shakers with Quinn, he'd given me one of his fuck-off attitudes, but on the other hand, he'd voted for me for team captain. At the moment, though, Chase was the least of my worries.

Ethan had said to give Quinn space, to let her be for a day or so then talk to her. But honestly, I didn't know if that would work because Tessa would always be a thorn, pricking and pricking and pricking until she got what she wanted. But she wasn't getting me, and it was high time she left Quinn alone. The million-dollar question was how to get Tessa to leave both of us alone.

I stared at my phone on the table Tessa had set up to sell the discount cards. I'd forgotten all about the fundraiser when I'd found out about my aunt Denise. But I was obligated to do my part for the team, even more so now that I was captain. I couldn't let them or Coach down.

I tapped out a text to Quinn. *Hey babe, can we talk?* I didn't know how much space I was supposed to give her, but if I didn't talk to her, I was going to flip out.

The noise in the rink grew louder with some of the fans screaming at the tops of their lungs at the game.

I couldn't help but remember how the fans at the basketball game the night before had been shouting with excitement every time we'd scored a basket. I'd been bummed I couldn't play. Yet watching Chase as point guard had been an eye-opener. He'd been great at that position. Maybe now I could have a shot at my sweet spot of shooting guard.

An older lady passed by, scanning the table and the sign we had posted. I set my phone down and straightened in the plastic chair.

Tessa piped up. "The cards are twenty dollars, and proceeds go to support our sports department at Kensington High."

We had the cards scattered around the table, and Tessa had

sprinkled gold stars here and there. She'd said something about making the table look inviting.

Whatever. I didn't want to be there. We had another thirty minutes before we closed up, or sooner if we sold all the cards. I counted five left on the table. Maybe the lady would buy all five.

To my dismay, she said, "I'll take two."

Tessa took care of the transaction while I again became fixated on my phone, waiting impatiently for Quinn to reply.

When the lady left, I spotted Celia at the concession stand. *What's she doing here?* Surely she wasn't there to spy on Tessa and me. Quinn would never do that. Tessa, on the other hand, would.

Celia bounced over, her dark-framed glasses sliding down on her nose as she held a drink in her hand.

Tessa sighed, or maybe groaned, as Celia approached. "Spying?"

"Are you into hockey?" I asked Celia.

Tessa giggled. "What he said."

Celia sipped on her drink. "I'm doing another sports article for the school newspaper."

"The hockey team has nothing to do with our school," Tessa fired back.

Celia gave Tessa a cocky smirk. "But it does." She pointed out at the ice. "See number fifteen in orange and black? He goes to our school. You know him, Tessa. Dustin Lane. Your old boyfriend. The same boy you continue to drool over."

Interesting. I assumed the teams were made up of older men, but upon a closer look, I realized some of the guys were young, as in my age or a little older. Maybe Tessa was only using me if she was trying to make her ex jealous.

"Have you forgotten, Tessa, that Dustin plays for Kensington?" Celia said more than asked.

I didn't know much about hockey, but I'd seen a couple of

games on TV. My fourteen-year-old brother, Marcus, had recently expressed interest in the sport after watching an NHL game on TV.

"Whatever," Tessa said.

Celia slurped the contents of her drink. "Maiken, have you talked to Quinn today?"

I hadn't since she'd left Shakers the night before with Chase. "Not yet. Is she okay?"

·Celia hiked her shoulders. "You should call her."

"Trouble in paradise?" Tessa's voice hitched as she swiveled in her seat.

Run, dude. Run far away.

"Not at all." Boy, that was a big, fat lie.

Celia scrunched her nose at Tessa. "Maiken isn't into you. So don't get your hopes up."

Tessa stood, smoothed her hands down her leggings, and poked out her chest. "We're working. So leave. We don't need you causing trouble or spying on us."

Celia threw her head back and laughed. "I don't spy. That's something you would do, though."

Tessa stuck her hands on her hips as she circled the table. "I would trust my boyfriend."

I pushed to my feet. "Tessa, I'm leaving. You can sell the rest of the cards."

She whipped her head at me. "What? You can't leave."

Watch me. "Here's the thing. I'm tired of your attitude. It sucks. It zaps the life out of a person. You can't come between Quinn and me. And stop bullying her. It's low and not cool. And this is the last time we work together." I grabbed my coat and stalked out. I wasn't waiting for her to cry or plead or say something sarcastic.

I'd barely gotten out the door when I heard Tessa's voice right behind me. "I'm telling Coach."

I pivoted so hard on my heel, I almost slipped on the icy pavement.

Celia was right on Tessa's butt.

I clenched my jaw as I came to a stop a foot away from Tessa. "You can tell Coach anything you want. I. Don't. Care. And whether Quinn beats you at ice-skating or not, you'll honor the deal you both made. You know why? Because the next time you spread a rumor about Quinn or do anything to embarrass her or hurt her, I will spread rumors of my own about you." I'd never been into gossip or drama at any school. Frankly, I stayed far away from all that. But I was willing to get my feet wet if it meant getting Tessa off my back and Quinn's.

"No one will believe you," she said in a defiant tone.

"Do you want to take that chance?"

Tessa pursed her lips as steam came out of her nose.

Celia's mouth was hanging open, although her wide eyes were cheering me on.

I left Tessa standing in the freezing cold as I hoofed it to my car. Adrenaline spiked through me faster than an F5 tornado. Within twenty minutes, I was ringing the doorbell at Quinn's house. As I waited for someone to answer, I suddenly got cold feet. What if she didn't want to see me? That would kill me. I checked the time on my phone. It wasn't too late, but her parents might think otherwise.

Mrs. Thompson answered, and her brown eyebrows lifted slightly.

"Is Quinn here?" I was certain she was.

She frowned. "It's not a good time."

I dropped my head briefly. "I won't be long."

"I'm sorry, Maiken. It's a school night." She had that motherly tone, but underneath, a thread of disappointment came through.

I fidgeted where I stood on the wooden porch. Arguing with

Mrs. Thompson wouldn't get me far, and I didn't want her to slam the door in my face.

"I texted Quinn earlier, but she hasn't responded. Please tell me she's okay."

She held up her finger. "Wait a second." Within a beat, Mrs. Thompson came out, shrugging into a bulky sweater. She closed the door behind her. "I know you adore my daughter. I know both of you are finding your way through how to date. I know high school isn't easy when it comes to the social aspect. Frankly, the high school environment is probably more difficult than when I went to school. But when you're in a relationship, both parties have to communicate. Do you understand?"

"Yes, ma'am." While I truly did, neither Quinn nor I communicated. "Quinn told you what happened?"

She wrapped her bulky sweater tighter around her. "I'm not sure she told me the whole story. Regardless, I know feelings are involved. You're a good boy, Maiken. You're going through some hard times, and if now isn't the right time to be dating my daughter, then I want you to tell her before the relationship gets even more serious."

Whoa! Who said it wasn't the right time? I'd never wanted to get involved with girls before Quinn. I'd always believed that girls were a distraction. But Quinn wasn't a distraction. Quinn was everything. Maybe I was crushing hard. Maybe I was naive to all the dating stuff and rules. But one thing I knew was that I wouldn't give up on Quinn and me.

You might move at the end of the school year. There was that. But that wouldn't be my choice.

"Mrs. Thompson, I have no intentions of breaking up with Quinn. Her and I had a misunderstanding. That's all." I'd seen my parents argue, and it wasn't like they'd split up over a misunderstanding. Granted, Quinn and I weren't married, but couples fought and made up.

She shivered. "Good to know."

I tucked my hands into my coat pockets. "Is she okay?"

Mrs. Thompson smiled. "She will be. Head home. It's late, and you can talk to her tomorrow."

Every bone in me screamed that I should protest, argue, and run into the house to find Quinn. But I was thinking with my heart and not my head.

Using your heart as a guide is the best way to say what you feel and show how you feel, but not at the expense of disrespecting an elder.

I inched down the porch steps, taking my time. Maybe on a whim, Mrs. Thompson would have a change of heart before I reached my car.

But as I climbed in, she went into the house and shut off the porch light. I scanned the farm, homing in on the barn, but even it was dark.

Sighing, I prayed Quinn and I could work things out.

Chapter 14

Quinn

I peeked out the window of Carter's room since it faced the driveway. Maiken sat in his Suburban, looking around. I couldn't see him that well, but it seemed like he was struggling to leave. I was tempted to disobey Momma and run outside, but she'd been adamant about me finishing my homework and resting my ankle. I'd been hobbling all day at school, and then I'd helped Daddy and my brothers with chores around the farm as best I could.

I'd strained to hear the conversation between Maiken and Momma, but all I'd heard was Momma telling Maiken I was okay.

I was far from okay. My heart hurt more than my ankle. I was glad I hadn't seen Maiken during school. I hardly did most of the time anyway since we had different schedules. If I had, I might have started crying, and with my luck, Tessa would've been around.

Maiken scanned the farm. I was sure he was wondering if I was in the barn. Daddy had closed up an hour ago. Sometimes we didn't get to chores until later in the evenings after dinner, but not that day.

The floor creaked outside Carter's room. "Quinn," Momma called.

I moved away from the window. "I'm in here."

She flicked on the light. "What are you doing in the dark?"

Maiken's engine fired to life.

I hunched my shoulders as my lips began to tremble.

She crossed the carpeted floor. "Oh, honey." She grasped my hand and guided me to Carter's bed.

After we were both seated, I stared at the poster of a red sports car over Carter's desk.

"It's time you told me what else is bothering you," Momma said.

I jerked my head, swallowing back tears. "What do you mean?"

"Quinn, a mother knows when something is wrong with her child. Sure, you told me you two had a fight. But is there more that you're not telling me?"

She'd always taught me that girls shouldn't throw themselves at boys. I was afraid she would be disappointed in me if I shared every detail.

"Do you love Maiken?" Her voice was soft.

I dashed a tear away. "I'm not sure. I think so." If the butterflies, giddiness, and the dire need to be with him all the time signified love, then I guess I did love him.

She tipped my chin up. "Look at me." Her tone bordered on concern. "Did you two have sex? Or is he pressuring you to have sex? Is that why he asked me if you were okay?"

I sucked in a choking breath. "What? No!" I shook my head hard from side to side. "No!" My cheeks were officially as hot as an inferno. Momma and I talked about a lot of things, but talking about getting naked with a boy was weird and, in another way, terrifying. Sure, Maiken and I kissed any chance we had, but him seeing me naked... I was not ready for that yet.

The wrinkles on her forehead disappeared as she sighed. "I want you to come to me before you get to that point."

The thought of my parents knowing I was going to have sex or did have sex was uncomfortable, embarrassing, and freaky.

"Momma, I'm not ready. Maiken isn't either." At least I didn't think he was.

She rubbed a hand over my cheek. "Do you know that for sure?"

My stuttering had tapered off around him, but if I brought up sex... Oh my God, my stuttering would probably go into the *Guinness Book of World Records.*

My head wouldn't stop shaking. "Momma, we haven't even said the word love, let alone talk about sex."

"First loves are extremely emotional, and those emotions can drive two people to make rash decisions without thinking. I want you to keep that in mind."

I wasn't naive enough to think that girls and boys didn't have sex in high school. I'd overheard some of the boys in class talk about their conquests, but I didn't want to be a conquest. I wanted to be special to a boy.

I wrung my hands in my lap. "You've told me that a girl's innocence is not something to give away to any boy." Those had been her exact words during our mother-daughter talk when I'd first gotten my menses.

She smoothed a hand over one side of her head, where strands of her brown hair had escaped her messy bun. "It's not. But because Maiken is your first love, you might think you want to experience everything with him. Please just come to me before you decide to have sex."

My face was still on fire, even more so when I thought about the time Maiken and I had had our first kiss in the boathouse. He'd walked away with an erection. Regardless, he would never pressure me into sex, nor would I pressure him.

I needed to get off the topic of sex. "Momma, I tried to kiss Maiken at Shakers last night, and he didn't want me to. I felt like he stuck a knife in my chest."

The creases on her forehead were back.

Yeah, I was a hussy as Granny liked to call a girl who was forward with boys.

"Did he tell you why?"

I bowed my head. "Yes." I inhaled. "He didn't like that I was trying to use him to m-make Tessa m-mad."

"I see," she said softly despite her lips forming into a thin line. "It proves my point that you're letting your emotions drive how you act. I taught you better than that. I expect you to apologize to him."

"I plan to." I was trying to get over my humiliation first, which I didn't think would go away anytime soon.

"It's getting late, and your brothers and father will be back soon." She rose. "Come on."

We both left Carter's room. She headed downstairs while I limped to my room on the other side of the hall. I wasn't using the crutches around the house. It had been difficult to climb the stairs, so I was careful not to put too much pressure on my left foot.

"Quinn," Momma called. "Let Brianna know that you're not skating on Sunday."

I held on to the doorjamb of my room. "Why not?"

"Look at you. Reschedule it." Then she padded down the stairs, the wood planks creaking under her feet.

Brianna wasn't going to like that. She and Celia had gone through a lot of trouble to set up the skate-off. But the more I thought about it, the more I didn't want to skate anyway. However, I'd made a deal with Tessa. If I backed out, she would scream forfeit and walk away with the notion that she'd won.

Let her. She isn't going to stop bullying you. So it doesn't matter.

Maybe it didn't. But it would certainly feel good to beat Tessa on the ice, something I hadn't been able to do.

I flopped down on my bed and stared up at the stars that were glued to the ceiling from when I was a little girl. Daddy had asked a couple of years ago if I wanted a fresh coat of paint. I didn't. I liked to stare at the fake sky when I was lying in bed at night. I puffed out my cheeks and released air like a blowfish. My phone rang, interrupting my thoughts.

I saw on the display that it was Celia, so I answered. "What's up?"

"Ohmigod," Celia practically shouted through the phone. "You are not going to believe what happened. Maiken and Tessa got into a fight, and he told her in so many words to leave you alone. It was classic, and I should've recorded it. But I was in shock at how Maiken seemed so... so... I don't know the word. Are you there?" She was vomiting words.

I laughed. "Breathe. Now slowly from the top. Word for word."

After her audible intake of air, she continued. "Maiken said, 'I'm tired of your attitude. You can't come between Quinn and me. This is the last time we work together.' That was inside the rink. Then outside, he practically got in her face, and it went something like this: 'Whether Quinn beats you at ice-skating or not, you'll honor the deal you both made. You know why? Because the next time you spread a rumor about Quinn or do anything to embarrass her or hurt her, I will spread rumors of my own about you.' Awesome, right?"

Euphoria, exhilaration, and vindication plowed through me, spiking my adrenaline, making me feel warm and special. My brothers had stood up for me many times, but not against Tessa or a girl. They'd been worried about boys. Sure, Celia had put in her two cents on my behalf, but it felt different to have my boyfriend stick up for me.

"How did Tessa react to all that?" I thought I knew.

"She was a first-class bitch," Celia said. "Has Maiken called you?"

"He texted me, and he also stopped by a few minutes ago, but my mom wouldn't let him in. School night and all."

"Talk to him, Quinn," Celia said in her friendly but not-so-friendly tone.

"I'm just mortified that I tried to use him."

"Normally, guys wouldn't mind if a girl used them. Kissing is hot," Celia said. "But I guess I can understand where he's coming from. Just talk to him. Clear the ice, so to speak."

I planted my feet on my bed with my knees toward the ceiling. "Speaking of ice, I can't skate on Sunday."

"What! We've sold tickets to this shindig."

I pulled the phone away from my ear briefly. "Sorry. Mom's orders. Can we do it the following weekend?" I had a feeling we couldn't because Brianna would have to reschedule the rink, and her dad had a business to run. "Or what do you think about using the Maxwell lake instead of the rink? I would just have to get approval from the Maxwells."

"Ooh, I like that idea," she said. "And I think Brianna will too. She said something about how the equipment that makes the ice has been acting up lately."

Regardless of the equipment, I preferred the lake for the simple reason that I enjoyed the outdoors and the feel of the wind on my face. I also felt like I skated better outside than in a rink.

On second thought, the Maxwells might not like a ton of kids in their backyard, although they had plenty of room. "How many tickets have you sold? That way, I can let them know what to expect."

"We've sold thirty. We're closing sales on Friday."

"I'll ask the Maxwells."

But at the moment, skating was the least of my worries. I had a relationship to mend.

Chapter 15

Maiken

The decibel level in the gym was at an all-time high. The fans were going crazy as we battled for baskets against Forest Grove. They'd been the ones we'd played during our very first game of the season, the same game in which I'd made a spectacle of myself by punching Chase.

However, the atmosphere at this game was different. Our team was different. I was different. Chase was too. We had thirty-five seconds left in the game—thirty-five seconds to either tie the game with a basket or win with a three-pointer.

"Time out," Coach called.

Coach Dean had been able to make it to the game. His sister-in-law had finally made it to town to help take care of his wife, who was home resting from a successful surgery. In the locker room before the game, Coach had shared with us that there'd been a good chance his wife had cancer. But tests had shown that the tumor they'd found in her uterus was benign.

I'd hoped for the same fate for my aunt Denise, but her cancer wasn't benign. Mom had updated us the night before that Aunt Denise was going through several rounds of chemo, but she was strong and in good spirits.

The team gathered around Coach and Kade.

Kade got out the clipboard and took control of the time-out. "Okay, we have thirty seconds on the shot clock and the ball. Use as much of those seconds as we can. We need one basket to tie and a three-pointer to win. Chase, you've been on fire this game, scoring every time you shoot, but we need a three-pointer. So once the ball is inbound, get it to Maiken. I want to see a two-three zone." Kade drew the play out on the clipboard. "Liam and Woods, make sure you're guarding the net."

Everyone nodded in agreement.

It was the first day in a long time that I felt like I was on top of the world out on the court. The last time I'd felt I could do anything was the last game of the season at my previous high school. Dad had been in the stands, along with my whole family, and I'd been on fire that night, scoring twenty-five points in the game, most of them three-point shots.

Tonight, I wasn't scoring all that much, but I was playing shooting guard, and that alone made me feel like I was back on track with basketball.

"I'm proud of you guys," Coach said. "Let's keep up the momentum."

I swung out my arm into the center of the circle. "All right, guys. Bring it in."

Chase placed his hand on mine, and the rest of the team joined in.

"We can win this game. On three," I said.

I counted out three, and in unison, we shouted, "Teamwork." Coach had been drilling that into our heads forever. As captain, I felt it was only appropriate to use that word for motivation.

Coach had a grin the size of California.

The ref blew the whistle. All of us jogged out with some of the guys adjusting their shirts. I scanned the bleachers. I would've given anything to have seen my dad cheering with all my siblings or even holding my mom's hand. But I believed he was watching over me. I believed he was with me every step of the way.

I smiled at my brothers and sisters, who occupied most of the second row. My brothers, Ethan, Marcus, and Jasper, leaned on their elbows. They nodded as if to say, "you got this."

The rest of my siblings were chatting while Harlan was trying to wiggle out of Lacey's lap. Lacey moved his curly brown hair out of his eyes and said something in his ear.

I was amazed at how great Lacey and Kade had been as pseudo parents, making breakfast, shuffling the little ones to school, meeting for after-school activities, cooking dinner, and helping with homework. It was almost as if they had kids of their own. Not only that, Lacey had never once looked tired or like she was ready for Mom to return.

Harlan waved with both hands. I couldn't help but smile and return the gesture. If anyone resembled my dad, it was Harlan, and because of that, a warm feeling traveled through me. Then I set my sights on Quinn, who was sitting in front of Lacey. That warmth grew hotter, but I tamped it down.

I'd been late to school that morning because the alarm hadn't gone off. My plan had been to get in as early as possible so I could talk to her before school started. But in hindsight, it was best that she and I talked away from school. With my luck, Tessa would eavesdrop, then rumors would spread. Quinn and I didn't need the hassle, nor did I need Carter in my face, although he'd been nonexistent since Mr. Thompson had given me his blessing to date Quinn. Besides, Brianna was taking up all Carter's time according to Liam.

Chase stood on the sideline, ready to inbound the ball. Liam, Woods, Miller, and I jockeyed into position with Miller trying to get free so Chase could pass him the ball. I hovered around the key, making sure I was primed for a three-pointer.

The ref blew his whistle, and the gym exploded with shouts and cheers. I zoned them out as Miller caught the ball. Chase darted in, and Miller's only option was to pass to Chase. The redhead guarding me kept blocking me from Chase.

Chase had no option but to pass to Liam, who had two guys on him. Woods darted around his opponent, and Liam passed the ball to him. I ran to the side of the key when Woods fired the ball at me just as Big Red came my way.

I faked left but went right. Big Red stayed left for a split second, and that second was too long.

I bounced the ball once as I positioned my feet outside the key, and in one fluid motion, I shot the ball. Holding my breath, I watched the ball hit the backboard, then the rim. And just when I knew I'd failed, the ball rolled in. It was as if some imaginary person had tipped it into the net.

Before I knew what was happening, Chase's arms were around me. "I've never been so fucking excited in my life," he screamed in my ear.

Everyone was trying to get a piece of me. Within seconds, the court was packed with Kensington fans. Liam's arms were pulling me when hands landed on my thighs.

I shrugged out of Liam's hold as best I could and found Harlan hugging my leg.

I picked him up. "Hey, buddy. What a game!"

"Awesome," he said.

Man, talk about a wonderful feeling. It was all I could do not to bawl my eyes out. In a weird sort of way, I felt like my dad's arms were around me.

Kade and Coach rallied the team so we could exchange handshakes with our opponents. I handed Harlan to Lacey as I joined the line.

"Nice shot," Big Red said to me, followed by all the other players on the rival team.

Yeah, I was on top of the world. Only one other thing would make my night epic. Once people started to scatter, I searched for the girl with butterscotch hair. I didn't have to look far. She crossed the court, heading in my direction. She had no crutches, a slight limp, wide eyes, hair spilling down around her shoulders, and a smile that sent my heart to the moon.

A hand touched my shoulder from behind before Lacey's voice was in my ear. "Invite her to dinner at the house. It should be ready in about an hour or so."

I'd told Lacey what had happened with Quinn. It had been hard not to. When I'd gotten home from Quinn's the night before, Lacey was in the kitchen, getting the kids' lunches ready for the next day.

"First fights are rough," she'd said. "Kade and I's first fight was a doozy, or was it our second? Anyway, makeups are the best."

I hoped she was right.

Lacey hurried off, chasing Harlan.

Then the bane of my existence ran over, beelining for either Quinn or me. Tessa batted her lashes at me. "Great game, Maiken. Too bad you won't be here next year. I heard you're moving."

The color drained from Quinn's pretty face, and I wanted to sew Tessa's lips together. Not only that, either the girl hadn't heard what I'd said to her, or she didn't care about the threat. "Did you forget our conversation at the rink?"

She stuck her hands on her hips. "Oh, I heard you loud and clear."

Don't fuel her fire, dude. But it was too late. "I was serious about spreading rumors of my own about you."

"Nothing you spread would bother me," she said with a flippant attitude.

Quinn snarled at her. "I could tell everyone your ex got you pregnant last year."

For the first time, fear crossed Tessa's face. "That's not true." Steam came out of her nostrils.

For some reason, I believed Quinn. Maybe because Tessa was turning a dark shade of red.

"Maybe not," Quinn said. "But you know how kids in school believe every rumor."

Tessa huffed. "You know, Quinn, our deal is off."

"So I won," Quinn said in a soft voice.

"Maiken," Liam called. "Locker room."

I tossed a look over my shoulder. The team was filing out of the gym. "I'll be there in a sec." I was about to grab Quinn's hand and rescue her when Brianna and Celia came out of nowhere.

Tessa studied Quinn with a furious intensity. "You haven't won shit."

"Just the two ladies I want to see," Brianna said, oblivious to the tension.

I was out of there. But first, I snagged Quinn. "She'll be right back." I guided her toward the exit at the same time Chase poked his head in.

"Maxwell, come on. We're all waiting for you."

"I'm coming," I said to Chase before regarding Quinn. "Would you like to come over for dinner tonight? Say in an hour?"

"Okay," she said with a half smile. "I'll have Celia drop me off."

Without thinking, I leaned down and kissed her quickly on the lips.

She froze.

Before I could read anything into her stiff lips, I said, "I'll see you later." Then I jogged out. Within a minute, I barreled into the locker room full of shouts and excitement. The guys were high on adrenaline for sure.

"There he is," Woods said, swiping a towel over his blond hair.

"Speech," Liam shouted as he tore off his jersey.

I'd never been a leader, but my dad had always believed I had it in me to lead a team. But I wasn't the one who'd won the game. I stood up on one of the benches. Making speeches in the locker room was becoming a habit.

I swiveled my head around the room. "Listen up. First, great teamwork. You guys played your asses off. You're the ones who deserve the credit." I sought out Chase, who was standing against a locker across from me. "Chase, dude, you're the MVP of this game. You brought this team together." That was the truth. He'd done more than he had in the last two games, and frankly, I would've sworn I was looking at a different guy.

He waved his hand around. "All of us put in the hard work. But I think I found my position. Honestly, I never thought I could do as good a job as Alex at point guard."

"You were made for it, man," Miller shouted.

Chase considered me. "Maxwell, is it true you'll be moving at the end of the school year?"

All heads rounded on me, and the sound in the locker room died. Only my family knew we might move. Well, Quinn did too. But it wasn't as if I were keeping it a secret. What the next school year held for me was up in the air.

I swallowed the elephant in my throat. I hated to disappoint the guys. We were starting to gel as a team—a team that could be awesome and win championships.

Kade came in, standing near the entrance to the bathroom area.

"Well, are you moving?" Woods asked.

I looked at Kade as though he could give me the answer, but I knew he couldn't.

He just nodded.

I wasn't sure what to make of that, but the guys needed to know. "I can't answer that." I made a point to lock eyes with each of them. Then I filled them in on my aunt Denise. "Look, guys. Let's not let the fact that I might move ruin the rest of our season. We have a good shot to go to the playoffs."

Kade crossed large arms over his chest. "He's right. Let's keep up the momentum. Coach and I will see you at practice tomorrow."

Excited chatter ensued as the guys changed and talked about the game.

I went over to my locker. "Chase, where did you hear that rumor?"

He lifted his foot up on the bench to untie his shoe. "Tessa overheard your sister telling a friend in the cafeteria. I figured it was true if it came from a good source. Sorry about your aunt too."

I peeled off my uniform. "Thanks, man."

I hoped I could continue to play for Kensington next year and the year after. But my sole focus at the moment was Quinn. So I got my butt into gear.

Chapter 16

Quinn

An hour and a half later, Celia was pulling into the Maxwell estate. I was thirty minutes late, thanks to Tessa and the heated discussion we'd had over the darn skate-off.

Tessa didn't want to reschedule. "Either skate, or I win," she'd said in her venomous tone.

I'd almost forfeited. But Celia and Brianna had worked hard to set up everything and sell tickets. I couldn't and wouldn't let them down. Besides, I'd made the deal. I had to see it through.

"Don't forget to ask if we can have the competition here," Celia said as I opened the passenger door.

I nodded and jumped out.

"Oh, and Quinn, have fun making up with Maiken."

Grinning, I dashed up to the front door, my belly swirling with excitement. Honestly, nothing mattered much anymore except Maiken. I would be devastated if he moved away. I would die a thousand deaths for sure.

Think positive.

The door opened before I could ring the bell.

Emma flicked her brown hair off her shoulder. "I saw you through the window.

I stepped in, and we exchanged a hug. I hadn't had a chance to say much to her at the game. She'd been busy watching her younger sisters. "It's great you're back."

"So, about this skate-off," she said. "What can I do to help? Are you going to practice on the lake? I got skates for Christmas, you know."

I let out a small laugh. "Slow down."

Lots of squealing and giggling filtered out of the living room off the foyer.

"Maiken has been playing with Charlotte and Harlan since he got home."

I peeked in. A fire crackled in the fireplace as Charlotte, Harlan, and Maple climbed on top of Maiken, tickling him.

Maple hopped off, her sandy-blond pigtails swinging in the process. "Quinn," she cooed.

At the mention of my name, Maiken lifted his head. "Okay, guys." He tried to get up, but Charlotte, the nine-year-old, protested.

"Pizza is here," Lacey shouted.

I guess I wasn't as late as I'd thought.

Emma extended her hand. "Come on, kids. Let's eat."

"Quinn and I will be there in a minute," Maiken said to Emma.

Harlan ran up to me. "Hi, Quinn." His curly mass of hair was all over the place.

I couldn't help but smile, which was a stark contrast from earlier when Harlan had had me on the verge of tears. He'd run out on court after the game and into Maiken's arms. The brotherly love between them was so sweet and intense that Lacey had had tears in her eyes.

Wrangling in the kids, Emma said, "Don't take too long, or else all the pizza will be gone."

With a family of eight kids, I would imagine she was right.

Maiken lazily raked his gaze over me. His cheeks were red, and his hair was a mess.

My breathing ramped up, and my pulse followed suit. I stabbed a thumb at the foyer. "M-maybe we should join the crowd."

He stalked toward me, his bare feet sinking into the thick white carpet as he closed the distance between us.

I licked my dry lips as my emotions wreaked havoc inside me. Suddenly, I had the urge to shout to the world that I loved Maiken Maxwell.

I dared not share that yet. What if he didn't say it back or didn't feel the same way? I couldn't risk having my heart sliced and diced like a tomato on a cutting board.

My panic was short lived when Maiken's warm, large hands landed on my cold cheeks, which were heating up now that his lips were an inch away from mine.

"I'm sorry," he said.

"I'm the one who's s-sorry. I overreacted, and I shouldn't have used you to get to T-Tessa."

"That night at Shakers, I wanted to kiss you so badly. Don't ever think that I don't." Then his lips were on mine—warm and soft.

I sucked in a breath, and when I did, he pushed his tongue in. An explosion of stars coated my vision as I returned the kiss.

The voices in the house dulled as I wrapped my arms around his neck and deepened the kiss. I wanted to stay like this forever.

He broke away. "We should stop." His voice sounded strained.

All I could do was nod as Momma's words blared in my head. *First loves are extremely emotional, and those emotions can drive two people to make rash decisions without thinking.*

"So no crutches?" he asked with pinched features.

"My ankle is a little better, but I have it wr-wrapped pretty tight right now."

"What about skating?"

"We're postponing the skate-off for a week to help my ankle heal, but Brianna is unsure if she can get the rink again."

He held my hand as we headed to the kitchen. "Why don't you use the lake?"

Surprise fluttered through me, making me angle my head. "I was going to ask Kade that very thing?"

He gave me a blushing grin. "Great minds."

"Ask me what?" Kade asked behind me.

I didn't hear his footsteps. Nevertheless, I turned around.

Kade stood tall. His hair was damp, and his copper eyes were prodding me.

The three of us entered the kitchen amid a flurry of giggles, hands grabbing pizza, and a couple of burps from the boys. I explained to Kade what we had in mind and that the head count was probably thirty or so kids.

Kade joined the kids at the island. "No problem. We've had parties at the lake a few times. Haven't we, Lace?"

Lacey blew hair from her forehead as she wiped Harlan's mouth. "They were doozies too."

"It's not a party," I said. "Tessa and I will be skating."

Emma chewed on her pizza at the island. "Who's judging the competition?"

I'd learned earlier that the plan was to have the crowd cast votes. "The people who bought tickets."

Ethan snagged a pizza from one of eight pizza boxes that were spread out over the island. "I'm going down to the family room to watch TV with Marcus and Jasper."

"Wait," Lacey said. "Take more pizza."

On Ethan's way out, he clapped his free hand on Maiken's shoulder. "Great game, bro. I'm proud of you." Then he was gone.

Maiken and I found two empty barstools and sat down to eat. It was officially a great night. I'd made up with my boyfriend. Kade had given us the thumbs-up to use the lake. Now all I needed to do was practice my skating routine. Hopefully, my ankle would cooperate.

Chapter 17

Maiken

Four days had passed since Quinn and I had kissed and made up. Since then, we hadn't had a chance to spend any time together. Kade still had me coming home from school right after practice and doing my homework, although I'd been procrastinating on writing the poem I had due for English that week.

I stared at a blank piece of paper, wiggling the pen in my hand. Maybe with the tsunami of a snowstorm raging outside my bedroom window that Sunday, school would be canceled the next day. Snowstorm or not, I had to come up with a poem. I laughed. I wasn't a writer.

You may not be, but think of something, or else you'll fail English. I couldn't let that happen. I was the captain of the basketball team. As their leader, I had to be the model student. "Lead by example" had always been my dad's motto.

I kicked out my legs, snagged my phone, and texted Quinn:

What are you doing? I miss you.

I hadn't been able to see her on Saturday because of the weekend blizzard that had kept everyone inside.

A knock sounded at my door before Emma came in. "Movie starts in ten."

I pushed to my feet. "A movie is better than English."

She sat on Ethan's bed.

With all my siblings back in Ashford, we were once again living in Uncle Martin's home since the one Kade and Lacey had been living in was too small for eight kids and two adults.

A sour expression crossed Emma's face. "I talked to Mom."

A prickly feeling spread over my skin. "Is everything okay?"

She slumped her shoulders. "We shouldn't be here. We should be at Mom's side. She's been crying every night, Maiken. She needs help. She needs us."

My heart broke in two as I sat beside her. "I know, but we have school, and she can't take care of Aunt Denise with all of us there."

She fiddled with her fingers, something she always did when she was nervous or sad. "I know."

I draped my arm around her. "We'll get through this." I didn't believe my own words, but as a big brother, I had to instill some hope in her and all my brothers and sisters. I just didn't know how. I barely had any myself.

She rested her head on my shoulder. "Our lives are falling apart. Dad's death is really hitting me all of a sudden."

I pulled her tighter to me, and she started crying.

During all the craziness surrounding Dad's death and funeral, Emma had been the one to keep a smile on most of our faces.

She buried her face in my chest, her body shuddering as she let out all her pain. All I could do was shed tears as I rubbed her back.

Light footsteps resonated in the hall. "Emma. Maiken," Lacey said.

Emma pulled away, wiping away her tears.

Concern filled Lacey's bright-green eyes as she regarded us. "Is it about your mom? I'm sorry. I overheard you talking to her, Emma."

"That and our dad," I muttered.

Lacey smoothed a hand down her black leggings. "I have an idea. Bundle up. All of us are going for a hike."

"There must be like a foot of snow out there," I said.

"Snow isn't going to hurt anyone. Now get dressed." Her tone was firm. "We'll meet down by the garage in ten minutes." She left with determination in her step.

"What do you think?" Emma asked, downtrodden.

"I think we shouldn't get on her bad side."

Emma smiled for the first time since she'd walked in. "I think you're right. I'll go get dressed." She started for the door. "Maiken, I love you."

I choked back my emotions. "I love you too, sis."

My phone beeped with a text from Quinn.

Quinn: *My ankle is feeling much better. I was going to practice on the lake, but with the snow, I probably shouldn't. So I'm taking Apple out for a ride. She loves the snow. You could ride with me?*

Maiken: *LOL.*

Quinn: *I'm going to get you on a horse yet.*

Maiken: *Not today. We're going for a hike.*

Quinn: *Hike?*

Maiken: *Lacey has something up her sleeve. Not sure. But I'll call you later?*

She sent two heart emojis.

Fifteen minutes later, Lacey was holding Charlotte's hand on one side and Harlan's hand on the other as she led the way down toward the lake. Emma shuffled behind her, holding Maple's hand. Marcus, Jasper, and Ethan walked together in front of Kade and me. All of us were wrapped in hats, boots, scarfs, and winter coats.

The snow floated to the ground as Harlan talked animatedly about squirrels even though we didn't see any at the moment.

"Where are we going?" Emma asked.

"Just follow Lacey," Kade said.

We left the open landscape of the backyard and trudged into the woods. Trees towered over us, their branches creating a snow-covered canopy as though we were walking through a tunnel.

The path narrowed around the lake, causing us to file behind one another in twos. Before long, we left the tunnel of trees and were standing in a large open clearing with the lake on our right. The snow wasn't as high on that side of the lake. I suspected that the trees had captured most of the light, fluffy stuff.

Lacey ambled over to a large, flat rock that poked out of the snow. "Gather around."

It was then I remembered what Kade had told me about Karen's memorial.

Kade guided Harlan, Maple, and Charlotte until they were standing in front of the rock.

"What's happening?" Ethan whispered.

"You'll see." I found a spot behind Harlan, Maple, and Charlotte.

Jasper, Marcus, Ethan, and Emma followed.

Lacey cleared the snow off the rock, revealing the initials KM that were etched deep into the stone.

"I don't get it," Jasper, my thirteen-year-old brother, said. "You brought us all the way out here for a rock?"

"My thoughts exactly," Marcus muttered at Jasper's side.

"Jasper," Emma scolded. "Manners."

Kade, who was now beside Lacey, raised a hand. "It's okay. Lacey had a similar reaction when I first brought her out here."

Ethan settled on my right. "I hope this is good," he said in a low voice.

Lacey swung her gaze around. "When I met Kade, I was in a bad place in my life much like you. I was mourning the death of my mom and my sister. I had just moved to town. I was new in school, and being a female baseball player, I made enemies. It seemed nothing was going right for me."

Kade tugged his wife to him as she continued.

"Honestly, if it wasn't for Kade showing me Karen's memorial, I'm not sure I would've healed as fast as I did. Don't get me wrong —I think about my mom and sister endlessly. But I don't think of how they died. I think of how they lived. I remember all the good times we had, the laughs, the vacations, and fun we had. Your dad was a very special person."

Maple, my eleven-year-old sister, sniffled. "We miss him."

Charlotte knelt down in the snow and touched the flat stone. "I talk to my daddy every night while I'm in bed."

Lacey mimicked Charlotte's position on the other side of the rock. "What do you talk about?"

"I tell him about my day, and I tell him when Harlan is bad."

Most of us laughed at the last part.

Harlan followed suit. "I do too."

That got another round of laughter.

Lacey rose, adjusting her hat over her ears. "I brought you out here to show you how Kade and his brothers remember their sister. This is their place to connect with Karen, to talk about the good times, to laugh at something she said or did. It's their way of celebrating and honoring her life."

"Rather than mourn," Kade said. "I want all of you to think of a way to celebrate your dad. Decide on something together. It doesn't have to be right now, but talk about it as a family."

"We're never in a place long enough to do something like this," Emma said.

"I'm sure we will be soon enough." I punched as much confidence as I could into that line. We didn't know what next year would bring, but I sure prayed Ashford would be our home.

I agreed with what Ethan had said to me. *"We can't keep moving. We can't keep leaving friends behind."* I couldn't leave Quinn or basketball. Not only that, all of us had to feel like we belonged somewhere. We couldn't keep living like gypsies. Otherwise, we would never heal.

"Never forget we're family." Lacey's voice made me blink. "We're here for you."

Marcus, who looked more like me with his blue eyes, knelt down near Charlotte, swiping his hand over the flat rock. "Why are there five hearts underneath Karen's initials?"

Kade gave him a wide grin. "She loved hearts, and each heart represents a sibling—Kelton, Kody, Kross, Karen, and myself. And Karen had a saying: 'A beating heart is the mystery behind a person. When people hurt, their hearts hurt. When they love, their hearts love, and when they cry, their hearts cry too. The heart knows everything.'" Kade cleared his throat on the last line. No doubt his emotions were tugging at him.

"That's super cool," Marcus whispered. "My heart hurts for Mom."

Tears streamed out of my eyes like a rushing waterfall. Ethan lowered his head. Emma cried softly. Jasper joined Marcus, Charlotte, and Harlan as they appeared to pray over the rock. Maple grasped my hand.

Silence hung in the air as emotions gripped each one of us. Even Kade had cloudy eyes as he held his wife tightly. Then he nodded at me as if to tell me it was time for me to speak.

Frankly, I had no words. All I kept thinking about was my mom and Aunt Denise. Sure, we needed to celebrate our dad, but like Marcus, my heart hurt for Mom. Emma was right—she shouldn't be shouldering the entire burden down in Georgia by herself. But she didn't need all of us in the way while she took care of her sister.

As if winter turned to summer in an instant, an idea popped into my head. But before I said a word, I had to make sure it was doable.

"We should head back," Kade said.

"Let's make some hot chocolate, and we can roast marshmallows in the fireplace," Lacey added.

Excitement stirred from most of the kids as they scurried to start walking back. Emma and Ethan began talking about the movies they wanted to watch.

I inhaled the clean, crisp air as I followed the group with Kade alongside me.

"What's on your mind?" Kade asked. "I can see the steam coming out of your head." He chuckled.

I glanced at Kade. "They have good doctors around here. Don't they?"

"Of course," he said. "Boston has some great doctors and hospitals. Why?"

I hunched my shoulders, slipping my hands into my coat pockets. The wind was brisk and brutal. "I was thinking that Aunt Denise could find a doctor here. That way, my mom could come home, and we could be a family, and we could help her."

"Mm," Kade said. "Brigham and Women's Hospital in Boston is one of the best for what your aunt is going through, although she might not want to leave Georgia."

I was going to ask my mom anyway. We needed her more than anything, and she needed us too. But as relief washed over me, tension wiped it away. "But where would we live?" I asked myself more than Kade.

His parents were due back from vacation at the end of the month. Their house was big, but all the beds were taken.

"Let's not worry about that," Kade said. "We'll figure all that out if your mom and aunt are open to the idea."

My mom would be worried about a place to live. She was grateful for my aunt and uncle's hospitality in letting us live with them until we got on our feet, but adding one more person to the family might not be something Uncle Martin would be amenable to.

Chapter 18

Quinn

Maiken chewed on a pen as he stared out the window from the couch in the boathouse. He was cramming for a chemistry test even though school had been canceled for the last three days. He seemed to be obsessed with studying. I couldn't blame him. I would be too if I were failing any class.

He grunted, a sound that reverberated through the small room.

Tying my skates, I peeked over at him.

His hair was disheveled from running his hands through it over and over since I'd gotten there. At the moment, he was rubbing his eyes like he was trying to take out his eyeballs.

"Need help?" I asked. I'd offered earlier, but he'd declined.

He slammed his chemistry book shut and opened a notebook. "Nah." He sounded weary. I couldn't tell if something other than school was bothering him.

Liam had told me about Maiken's speech in the locker room after the basketball game. The team had heard the same rumor as Tessa that Maiken could be moving. It was something I didn't want to think about. Maybe his mom had decided to stay in Georgia permanently and Maiken didn't know how to tell me. Suddenly, my stomach tumbled.

Maiken must've seen the panic on my face because he said, "It's okay. I have to write a poem, and I have no clue what to write."

Poems were hard to come up with. Stringing words together to rhyme, flow, and hold meaning was something I struggled with too. I could fly through math and science problems. But history and English? Not so much.

"Writing sucks," Ethan complained from his spot at the table where Emma was helping him with an English paper.

"I'm ready for a break," Emma whined. "I'm going with Quinn. I want to try my new skates that I got for Christmas."

And I had to test my ankle. I hadn't gotten on my skates since that first night I'd practiced at the rink, and if I were going to give Tessa a run for her money, I needed to practice, practice, practice.

The sun blared brightly, glinting off the ice, but we only had two hours at most before we lost the light. I strapped on my other skate. "Emma, we should get out there."

She didn't hesitate, scrambling to get her skates from her bag by the door.

Maiken hopped up. "I need some air."

Before long, all four of us were on the ice. Emma and I had on our skates, although she was a bit wobbly. Ethan and Maiken slid along on their boots, staying close to the boathouse.

But gliding around the ice wasn't going to help me win any medals. So I pulled Maiken. "Come on."

He didn't protest. "How's the ankle?"

I let go of him and spun around. "It feels fine. But the real test will be when I do one of my jumps."

"Let's see." His blue eyes sparkled until he scanned the lake, pensive and concerned.

I surveyed my surroundings, including the ice. "What is it?" I didn't see anything out of sorts. I usually checked the ice as I skated to make sure I didn't see any weak spots or cracks anywhere.

"I guess I can't believe I'm out in the middle of the lake." His tone was equal parts awe and fear.

I twirled around again to take in the serene view of snow-covered trees and the icy lake that spanned out far and wide. "I love it out here in the winter." I couldn't speak to summer since I'd had no reason to visit the Maxwells at that time. Although now that Maiken was living there, I might get the chance to swim in the lake.

Not if he moves. Shut up, I screamed at the voice in my head.

He tugged me to him. My body jerked, and I wobbled. In a flash, we were falling with me landing on top of him.

"Oh my God," Emma shouted.

Maiken laughed.

It took me a second to shake off the shock. "Are you okay?"

He clutched my hips. "Better than okay. I have my girl right where I want her."

A hot flush careened up my neck and settled in my cheeks. "I sh-should do a jump or something."

"Or I can kiss you," he said with a grin.

If the temps were twenty degrees, I couldn't tell. My face was burning up. "I might need one for good l-luck."

He raised the upper half of his body as I lowered mine. We met halfway, and just when I thought he would kiss me, he rested his forehead against mine. "You're absolutely beautiful, Quinn Thompson."

A rush of emotions crashed through me. I was falling for a boy who had a way of making me feel pretty, special, and confident.

I love you sat on the tip of my tongue, but I was afraid if I voiced those three little words that... I didn't know what would happen. *Would I scare him? Does he feel the same way?* Despite all that, I knew I would stutter so bad that *I love you* would sound foreign or unintelligible.

Silence froze us in place. If the ice was cold, I couldn't tell. All I could feel was Maiken's hot breath colliding with mine. We both seemed to be breathing a little heavier than normal.

"I think my butt is stuck to the ice," he whispered, breaking the spell.

I snorted then laughed. "We should get up." That was going to be an enormous feat for him rather than me. I could dig the toe of my skate into the ice for leverage, but he had nothing to anchor him except maybe me.

I motioned to get up, but he gripped my hips a little tighter. "Not so fast. I think you need a warm kiss for good luck."

I giggled, but the sound died when he captured my lips in his. The lake disappeared, as did Emma and Ethan.

His kiss was urgent, new, inviting, and had so much feeling behind it that a part of me knew he felt the same way as I did.

We kissed until Ethan's voice trickled in my ears. "Bro?"

I rolled off Maiken and pushed upright, steadying myself easily.

Maiken got on his knees, pressed his gloved hands onto the ice, and stood like a pro hockey player. "What is it?" Frustration rode Maiken's tone.

Emma was skating in circles near the boathouse, appearing to be in her own little world.

"I have a brilliant idea." Ethan's brown eyes were wide as though he'd found the answer to a complex math problem. "You know how Dad loved to fish? Why don't we get Uncle Martin to name his boat Harlan Marlin? Then this summer, we can take it out on the lake and celebrate Dad."

Maiken threw his arms around Ethan. "You're a genius."

Ethan shook hair from his forehead. "Do you think Uncle Martin would go for it?"

"Hell yeah," Maiken said.

I wasn't sure what was going on, but I liked the idea of them taking the boat out on the lake. That meant Maiken would be there during the summer.

Ethan and Maiken carefully made their way to Emma, and I decided it was time to do a few jumps and warm-ups.

While the three of them chatted, I stuck my earbuds in my ears and did a few warm-up laps.

The competition was T-minus three days. With Mozart playing and the wind whisking by me, I zoned out to everyone and everything. The good news about using the lake as our venue was that I could skate to music in my ears, which meant I wouldn't hear the crowd. That alone would keep me focused. I'd always had a problem letting the crowd get to me, especially after a fall when a collective intake of breath sounded like a bomb going off. That was always followed by complete and utter quietness that was louder than the people in the stands.

I skated one lap around, doing forward and backward crossovers. My ankle was in good shape. On my way out to the other end of the lake, I spiked my skate into the ice with one foot while jumping off the edge of my other foot. I brought my arms into my chest and followed through the mechanics. Then panic set in, causing me to fall on my butt as I came out of the jump.

Argh!

I could hear my former coach in my head. "Get up. Try again."

Like a robot, I got up and went around again. This time, I started with a simple one-legged spin, infusing a bit of flair and personality into it as though I were dancing ballet—soft and elegant.

As if the skating gods took control of my body, I dove into my old routine, not thinking about mechanics or if I had my arms pulled in tight enough or if I used the back edge of my skate or the toe pick. I just skated, using the large span of ice as I listened to Mozart.

Before long, I was jumping, spinning, and loving the freedom that skating gave me. I knew it sounded crazy, but skating felt like I was flying. Adrenaline rushed through me as I went in for a Salchow and landed perfectly like I had the previous three jumps. I finished with a sit spin, and when the music slowed, I spun my way up to standing position, angling my face toward the sky, my arms parallel to the ice as the music ended.

I stood in that position for a long minute, trying to catch my breath. On my last intake, arms went around my waist.

"You were amazing," Maiken said. "You're so going to win."

I righted my head, laboring for breath, but air in my lungs didn't matter. His infectious grin did, and I couldn't help but hug him so tightly, I was afraid I was cutting off his airway.

"I did it. I did it." That time I did squeal.

With him at my side, I could do anything. At least I prayed I could.

Chapter 19

Maiken

I wrote a poem. I, Maiken Maxwell, wrote a poem. Yep, I was surprised—or more like floored—at myself.

Watching the most gorgeous girl in New England skate had been my inspiration. Quinn Thompson belonged in the Olympics.

I'd been wrestling with words harder than a fighter in the ring. I could do many things, but writing wasn't one of them. A word problem in math was a breeze. But if I had to write a poem—bomb city.

But seeing Quinn skate had done something to my brain.

I hoped beyond hope that my English teacher would give me a C or better. I'd turned in the poem that Friday morning and had to wait until Monday for my grade.

Ethan lounged on the sectional sofa in the family room and had the TV remote primed to change the channel. "Are you going to read your poem to Quinn? Dude, I want to be there when you do." He was holding back another of his epic laughs. My brother had been ragging me since that morning on our way to school.

In my opinion, my poem was wicked lit. I hoped my teacher agreed.

I threw one of the couch pillows at Ethan from where I sat on the opposite end of the sectional. "Shut up. I should've never read it to you."

He held his stomach and roared with laughter. "How does it go again? Wait." He laughed harder. "You skate with heart. You skate with ease. You spin, you jump under the snow-covered trees." He was in tears.

I threw another pillow at him. "It must be good if you remembered it. Besides, if it gets me a C or better, I don't care if it sounds as corny as you say. Emma thought it was cute." I'd run the poem by her too.

He guffawed. "How does the rest go again?"

I flipped him off.

He pressed a button on the remote, and Netflix came on the screen. "You're so in love, it isn't funny."

"What is love? Do tell." I was being sarcastic as well as serious. Ethan was fifteen. He couldn't possibly know much about being in love, although he'd had a girlfriend before me.

"Pain." He spat out that word quickly.

"Love is pain?" I let that question simmer for a moment.

"Think about it," he said. "In some ways, love hurts so bad, it feels good. In other ways, love sucks when you have to leave someone behind. Either way, you're in pain. Just admit you love Quinn."

I let out a nervous laugh. My heart was telling me I did, but I wasn't ready to go down that path. "What if I tell her, and she doesn't love me? What if we move?" I was asking my younger brother for advice on love. *Go figure.*

He flopped his head against the couch. "Didn't Kade say the heart knows? So follow your heart."

I kicked up my feet onto the coffee table. "Did you ever tell Hannah you loved her?"

"Right before we moved here, I told her. But she didn't say it back. Instead, she said thank you."

I pinched my eyebrows. "What? Why?"

He frowned. "Girls can be weird, I guess. I've decided that I don't want a steady girlfriend."

"What changed your mind? I thought you wanted to find a girlfriend?"

"You and Quinn. I see how she looks at you, and I'm not ready for that intense feeling shit that comes with a girlfriend, especially if we move. 'Play the field' is my new motto."

I shook my head, grinning at the mere fact that we were young and naive when it came to girls and dating and everything else that came with that.

"Before long, you'll have all the girls in school vying for your attention," I teased.

"Dude, I already do. Freshman and sophomore girls are always trying to get my attention."

We both busted out laughing.

My phone rang, and Mom's name lit up my screen.

A trailer of some action flick on Netflix played on the TV screen.

"Kill the sound," I said to Ethan as I hit the speaker button on my phone. I'd been waiting for my mom to call, which was one of the reasons I hadn't gone to bed like the rest of the kids, although I could hear the pitter-patter of feet every now and then upstairs.

"Maiken." Mom's voice sounded as though she'd been crying.

"Is everything okay?" I asked.

Ethan slid down to be close to the phone. "Hi, Mom."

"Hi, sweetie. Any of the others with you?"

"It's just Ethan and me. Everyone else is upstairs, and I think Lacey is getting the younger ones in bed."

"How are Kade and Lacey holding up with eight kids?" she asked.

Ethan chuckled. "They're naturals. But we do want you to come home."

"Speaking of that…"

Ethan and I concentrated on the phone as though we were trying to pull Mom out from the other end.

"I thought about our conversation, Maiken. And you're right—Boston has a good hospital for Aunt Denise. But right now, she needs to stay here. She has a great doctor, and she's…"

I braced my elbows on my knees. "Mom?"

Sniffles came through the phone. "It's tough to see a loved one go through something like this."

Ethan hung his head. "I hate that we're not there with you."

"I know," she whispered. "But it's best if you're not."

Pain clutched my chest. It killed me that I couldn't do anything to take away the pain she was going through.

"What you can do for me is take care of each other, concentrate on school, and stay out of trouble."

Ethan and I did a double take at the phone.

"Who got into trouble?" Ethan asked.

"Kade tells me Marcus got into a fight at school."

That was news to me. Marcus hadn't shown any signs that he'd been in a fight, and he'd sat across from me at dinner. "I'll talk to him."

"Maiken," she said. "I know you feel like you have to, but let Kade handle it. Tell me about your day. How's basketball? How's Quinn?"

She was probably right to let Kade handle Marcus, but I was his big brother, and I felt like I needed to talk to him. "Our away game was canceled because of all the snow. And Quinn is fine." It had been two days since we'd hung out, although I'd seen her at school, and we'd texted earlier.

"He wrote a poem about Quinn," Ethan said matter-of-factly.

"Is that so? I would love to hear it."

Ethan nudged me, holding in a laugh. "I would too."

I shoved him, but he didn't move all that much. "It's kind of corny," I said to Mom.

"Please," she said.

I couldn't disappoint my mom. And maybe it would brighten her day. "I will if Ethan doesn't break out in hysterics."

"I won't," he said, not at all sounding convincing.

Here goes nothing. "You skate with heart. You skate with ease. You spin; you jump under the snow-covered trees. Elegant is a word to describe you. Beauty, grace, and fearless too. But words—words are but a tell, because it's you who has me under your spell."

Ethan's mouth formed into a tight grin. No doubt he wanted to let loose a laugh of all laughs.

"That is beautiful." Mom sounded so proud. "You never knew this about your dad, but he used to write me poems."

That got a raised eyebrow out of Ethan and me. At the same time, I took comfort that maybe my dad was really watching over me.

"Is Quinn's competition tomorrow?" Mom asked.

"Yes, ma'am," I said. "She's going to kill it too."

"Take pictures or maybe a video. I would love to see her skate."

Quinn was certainly a sight to see on the ice.

"Boys, I've got to run. I love you dearly. I'll call tomorrow."

Ethan leaned forward. "Mom, do you think we'll stay in Ashford?"

Silence hung in the air as I chewed on my finger.

"I can't answer that right now. When the time comes, I promise we'll talk about our living arrangements as a family. Sleep tight."

After Ethan and I said our goodbyes, Ethan said, "Limbo once again. I'm tired of it."

As a military family, our lives had always been in limbo, especially when Dad had been waiting on orders for his next assignment. So we should've been used to not knowing where we were moving or what lay ahead.

But I agreed with Ethan. I was tired of new schools, new friends, new everything. And now that I had a girlfriend, I refused to move.

Chapter 20

Quinn

Whether it was from the howling of the wind or the chatter of the people congregating just outside the boathouse, my stomach was in a tight knot. I ran to the bathroom as nausea threatened. Then I inhaled several times, looking at myself in the mirror. "I can do this. I can beat Tessa. I can jump. I can skate. Remember, put your earbuds in and let yourself feel the wind on your face as the music guides you. Don't look at the crowd. Don't think about how much better Tessa is than you."

I fluttered my shaking fingers through my hair before securing it in a ponytail with a band. I inhaled again then puffed out my rosy cheeks as I released all the air in my lungs.

"Quinn." Maiken called my name as the door to the boathouse opened and closed. "Are you in here?" His footsteps padded across the floor until he was standing in the doorway. His sandy-blond hair was unruly, which was a first for him. I suspected the wind had something to do with his hairstyle. Nevertheless, I liked the way his hair fell over his forehead with some strands covering one of his eyes.

"You're nervous," he said, leaning against the doorjamb casually, as if he didn't have a care in the world.

I would've given anything not to have nerves rifling through me like angry ants on a mission to find food for their queen.

I straightened, turning my attention to myself in the mirror. I was beyond nervous. "Did you kn-know that ants are on every continent on Earth e-except Antarctica?"

He didn't laugh but came to stand beside me, scanning my face in the mirror. "You've got this."

I bit a nail. "How do you know? You haven't seen Tessa skate."

His long fingers circled my wrist before guiding my hand away from my mouth. "I have something that might take your mind off the competition."

I didn't think kissing would work, but I was willing to give it a shot.

His blue eyes shimmered like shiny sapphires as we stared at each other. For a beat, his mouth didn't move, his body didn't move, and his hand was glued to mine.

Then his Adam's apple bobbed. "I wrote my poem."

Okay. I should've been happy for him. He'd struggled that day he had been studying in the boathouse. Yet from the scared expression on his face, I wasn't sure I wanted to hear what he had to say. Immediately, my mind drifted to him moving away. I couldn't figure out how my brain went from a poem to him moving, but it did. If he was planning on delivering bad news, then I had to stop him. I didn't want to know. I wouldn't be able to think let alone jump or spin or even stand up on skates.

He visibly swallowed. "Do you want to hear my poem?"

I nodded slowly.

He blew out a breath, his gaze riveted to me. "You skate with heart. You skate with ease."

My heart and stomach were doing front and back flips. He'd written his poem about me. *Oh. My. God.*

"You spin. You jump under the snow-covered trees." His chested lifted.

Mine did too.

Then he swallowed again. "Elegant is a word to describe you. Beauty, grace, and fearless too." He took another breath. "But words—words are but a tell. Because it's you"—he pointed at the mirror—"who has me under your spell." His expression was wary, his cheeks flushed.

My jaw nearly hit the tiled counter, and my eyes filled with tears. "Y-you wr-wrote that for m-me?"

His head bobbed. "You don't like it?"

Say something. Tell him how you feel. It seemed like the perfect time. My breathing ramped up. "I…" I licked my lips.

The door to the boathouse creaked. "Quinn," Celia called. "Tessa is here."

In an instant, the bubble that Maiken and I were under popped.

Celia stood in the doorway. "There you are. Enough kissy face. It's time to get serious. Tessa and Brianna are coming in. Maiken, out. We have business to take care of."

Normally, I would've giggled or rolled my eyes at my bestie, but I was a moment away from shouting at her to get out.

Maiken gave me a chaste kiss on the lips. "We'll talk later."

Yeah, we would.

Once he was gone, I sat down on the toilet. "You have the worst timing."

"Please tell me everything is okay between you two." Her businesslike demeanor vanished, and in its place was a softer voice—one that made my hands shake a little less.

"Of course. Why wouldn't it be?"

"The tension is dripping in here."

"He wrote me a poem."

She slapped a hand over her pink-stained lips. "Oh my God. Seriously?"

I was trying to recite it in my head, but I could only remember parts of it. I frowned.

She shook off her shock. "We'll take up this conversation later. I want to hear all about it. But right now, the topic is skating."

Brianna called out to Celia. "It's time."

Celia all but dragged me out of the bathroom.

Tessa and Brianna were looking around the boathouse in awe. The space had a manly vibe with a pool table, a foosball table, and even a card table.

Brianna took off her slouchy pink hat. "This is a great space to hang out in."

Tessa, who was dressed in black leggings, a black coat, and a red hat, studied a family picture of the Maxwells, one of many that hung on the walls.

"Whose kids are these?" She pointed at two little girls who had black hair much like hers.

I sidled up to her. "Kross Maxwell. That's Raven on the right and Reaghan on the other side of Kross." I knew it was Kross because of his large arms. I also knew the names of his daughters because my mom and Mrs. Maxwell were besties. I heard them talk all the time about grandchildren.

My mom had had Carter, Liam, and me a little later in life, so she wasn't in a rush to have grandkids.

"I want lots of kids someday," Tessa muttered.

"I haven't thought that far. I'll probably be in school forever since I want to be a doctor." It took me a moment to realize that we were actually being cordial and carrying on a normal conversation.

"You know this"—she wagged a finger between us—"doesn't mean we're friends."

And just like that, I came back to reality.

Brianna tapped on the pool table. "Let's toss a coin to see who goes first."

Tessa and I turned around and shuffled forward a couple of feet until we were at the pool table across from Brianna and Celia.

Celia played with a quarter. "Sadly, only fifteen people out of the thirty who bought tickets showed today. They'll be judging your performance. Stay within viewing distance. There's enough ice to do that."

Brianna wrinkled her nose. "The snow and cold I'm sure kept the rest of them away. We would've had a better turnout if the ice equipment at the rink didn't break."

"Should we cancel?" Tessa asked with a hitch in her voice.

She hadn't wanted to cancel before, but now she seemed apprehensive.

"No," I said in a brusque tone. I'd made myself sick over our deal, and we were going to see the competition through once and for all.

Celia snapped her fingers. "Focus. We're not canceling. After both of you skate, Brianna and I will tally up the votes."

Brianna turned serious, reminding me of my mom when she was about to reprimand me for something I'd done wrong. "I want both of you to consider something before you go out there. The deal is if Quinn wins, then Tessa, you'll stop bullying her. But if Quinn loses then it's status quo between you two. I don't see that as fair. Therefore, I want both of you to consider a truce no matter who wins. I want both of you to think about how you want to be remembered in high school. Bullying will not get you far in life."

"Says the girl who invented bullying at Kensington," Tessa responded harshly. "If I wanted to call a truce, I would've a long time ago."

"Don't forget, Tessa, I'm the one who will recommend you to

be head cheerleader next year. And don't think Ms. Tatum doesn't know you have a bad attitude."

Tessa didn't flinch. She only shrugged as though she didn't care what next year held for her. "No truce if Quinn loses."

No surprise there. But I remembered that Maiken had threatened Tessa. "Are you forgetting Maiken's words?" I asked even though I knew she would brush it off.

"Whatever," Tessa said.

Regardless of threats, truces, or bullying, I had to win. That was the best way to get Tessa off my back. Besides, Maiken couldn't get into any trouble or become a bully like her.

Celia held up a quarter. "Brianna and I decided that if the coin lands on heads, then Tessa will skate first."

Who went first didn't matter. What mattered was getting the show on the road so I could tell Maiken how I felt about him.

Celia tossed the coin in the air. The quarter flipped once then twice before it landed in the middle of the pool table on tails. "Quinn, you're up first."

Let the fun begin.

Chapter 21

Maiken

The wind whipped around like one of those hurricanes I'd been through in North Carolina. The only difference now was that the cold stung like a hard slap to the face. The snow that had accumulated in the backyard down to the lake was piled up in mounds near the garage. Kade had cleared the area for the competition.

Thick clouds floated above, and I wished the sun were shining. Maybe then I wouldn't have been shaking in my boots. Or maybe it wasn't the cold at all, but the way my pulse was racing after reciting my poem to Quinn. I honestly couldn't tell if she'd liked it or not.

She did, and you know it. The inflection in her voice said she was flattered. Even if that were true, I wanted to hear what she really thought.

Chase waltzed over, his hands tucked into his parka. The tips of his ears were red. "Maxwell."

We'd been pretty cordial to one another since our basketball game over a week and a half ago. We weren't friends and didn't hang out or anything. We just didn't snarl at one another anymore.

The fifteen kids who had purchased tickets were dressed in

layers and drinking hot chocolate, which Emma was serving from thermoses.

I blew into my gloved hands. "So who do you think will win?"

Chase hunched his shoulders. "No idea. My sister is good. That's all I know."

Even though I hadn't seen Tessa skate, my money was on Quinn.

"My sister will still be a pain in the ass even if she does lose to Quinn," Chase announced.

That wasn't a surprise. "No, she won't."

In slow motion, his head swiveled toward me. "Care to tell me how you know that?"

I raised my hands. As much as I would've liked to go a few rounds with Chase, I didn't want to ruin the progress we'd made. "Simple. She likes to spread rumors. I can too."

"Quinn's okay with you doing that?" Chase asked.

I could feel a deep crease forming in between my eyebrows. I'd never considered how Quinn would feel if I spread rumors about Tessa. In all honesty, it was only a scare tactic on my part, and I hadn't thought further than that. All Tessa needed to do was believe my threat, which she had, based on her shocked expression.

"You're concerned about Quinn?" Stupid question on my part. After all, Chase had a thing for Quinn. But Tessa was his kin.

"I like Quinn," he said. "You know that."

"And you try to step in my way any chance you get." Case in point was when he'd driven her home after our first fight at Shakers.

"I might be a dick, but I don't force a girl to like me."

My respect for him went up a notch. "Good to know. Look, man, your sister needs an attitude adjustment. So I hope she backs off even if she comes out of this competition the victor."

"Time will tell," he muttered.

The small crowd hooted and hollered when Quinn, Tessa, Brianna, and Celia came out of the boathouse. It was good to see that even with the cold temps, they were into the competition.

Quinn waved my way. Chase and I both returned the gesture at the same time.

"You can do this," Liam shouted from somewhere behind me before he was standing on my left. "Sorry I'm late." He stabbed a thumb over his shoulder. "Miller and Woods are with me."

Coach had said we needed to spend time outside of school doing something as a team. And since our two days at the farm, we hadn't done anything. As captain, I was classifying the skating competition as a team function.

Woods and Miller joined us.

"I can't believe I'm going to say this," Woods said on the other side of Chase. "But I think I would rather shovel horse manure than stand out in this freaking cold weather."

"Tell you what," I said. "When this is done, we can hang in the boathouse. There's a foosball table and a pool table. Plus heat."

"For real?" Chase asked. "I mean foosball table? I'll beat you guys hands down."

Miller, who was next to Liam, poked out his head. "We'll see about that."

Satisfaction made me grin. The five of us were gelling as a team. Hopefully, we could continue the high we were on for the next two years. But the possibility of moving to Georgia, or somewhere other than Ashford, swept away with the wind when Brianna and Celia addressed the crowd.

I tuned them out and focused on Quinn, who was rocking a pair of navy-blue leggings, a muted yellow sweater, a white ski jacket, and a pair of bright-yellow earmuffs.

Celia handed out a paper and pen to the fifteen judges, who took them and headed up onto the deck where they would have a better view.

"Quinn," Brianna said. "You're up."

Quinn removed her jacket and blade guards, put her earbuds in her ears, and walked out onto the lake. She skated backward for a few feet before she spun around and skated out. After a few warm-up laps, she stopped, tilted her back, and struck a pose, as if to say, "I'm a badass." Within a second, she started her routine.

After one lap around, she went in for her first jump.

"There she goes," Liam said. "Come on, sis. Stick it."

Holding my breath, I prayed she didn't fall.

When she came out of the jump, one leg went behind her and her arms swung out to the sides as she landed perfectly.

"Wow," Chase said. "She's awesome. Maybe she will beat Tessa."

I checked on Tessa, who was leaning up against the railing of the stairs. She too was watching as intently as the rest of us.

Quinn seemed to be in her element. She performed her one-legged spin, and when she finished, she skated around the ice, arms flowing like a scarf fluttering in the wind.

"Here comes another jump," Liam said. "I've watched her perform this routine so many times."

Again, I held my breath.

"This is a Salchow," Liam added.

Well, that Salchow was perfect too.

The guys hooted and hollered.

After one more jump and a sit spin, Quinn's routine ended. Not one fall. Not one error.

But I wasn't the expert, and neither were the kids on the deck. But if I were judging the competition, not knowing much about ice-skating, I would vote for Quinn.

Everyone clapped, but the sound was muffled with all of us wearing gloves.

Tessa nodded at Quinn as she came off the ice.

I rushed down to meet my girl, who was breathing heavily and smiling like she had won a gold medal.

I grabbed her jacket and held it open for her. "You were fantastic."

She slipped her arms in. "Thank you. I felt amazing out there. Now let's see how Tessa does."

I was actually interested in watching Tessa. Quinn had always bragged about how good Tessa was at skating. Even Chase had confirmed that.

I wrapped my arms around my girl, waiting for the show to continue.

Chapter 22

Quinn

I was floating on a cloud of happiness and content. I felt like I had skated the best performance of my life. I couldn't remember ever doing that well when I'd been competing.

"How's your ankle?" Maiken's hot breath on my ear made me quiver.

"Throbbing a little, but good." A twinge of pain registered now that I was standing idle.

Maiken pressed his head against mine so our cheeks were touching. I snuggled into him. My head was light, and my heart was swelling.

Tessa skated a few laps around the immediate area, constantly looking down at the ice as though she wasn't sure what to do.

"What's she doing?" Maiken's voice vibrated against me.

"I'm not sure. She looks timid."

"Is she okay?" a girl on the deck asked.

"I should go check." I left the warmth and gooeyness of Maiken and skated out.

Tessa lifted her dark gaze and stopped when she saw me, removing her earbuds. "I'm fine. It's eerie to be out here on this big lake."

I guessed the dread she'd had written all over her face when I finished my routine had had nothing to do with my good performance.

I agreed. I'd been apprehensive my first time skating on the lake. Even Maiken had found it weird to be standing in the middle of the lake.

I scanned the ice and the area around us. All the people on shore were watching in earnest. A gust of wind whipped by us, howling as it continued its path to the trees in the distance.

"Just imagine you're on the ice in the rink." That was what I'd done.

Her chest lifted. "What if the ice breaks?"

As long as I'd known Tessa, I had never seen her frightened, although when she'd fallen in the pool with me, she'd had a look of horror on her face.

"We've had consistently freezing temperatures." It had to be nineteen or lower.

In spite of the temps, sunny days would heat the water under the ice and, in turn, melt the ice from the bottom up. And we had had a couple of sunny days in the last week with temperatures maybe climbing above thirty-two. But I didn't think a day or two of thirty-five-or-so degrees would cause the ice to melt. The area from the boathouse out to the middle certainly appeared solid.

"I just skated on it and have been since early December. If you're worried, stay in this area." I waved my hand between the boathouse and us.

Steam floated out of her mouth as she blew out a breath. "I need more ice to do my triple axel."

Wow! She can do a triple axel. That was one of the hardest jumps in ice-skating. If she nailed it, I might have to vote for her. "Then skate out more and survey the ice." I didn't know what to tell her except... "If you're afraid, we can end this competition."

"Like hell." In a split second, her cocky attitude came back with a vengeance.

I clenched my jaw. "Then skate, or else I win." The girl made me want to drill a hole in the ice underneath her.

She fisted her hands at her side.

I wasn't waiting around for her to spit venom at me. So I stomped off then glided back to my boyfriend, who was flanked by Chase and my brother.

"Is she okay?" Chase asked.

"Peachy." I snuggled back into Maiken's arms. The high I'd had earlier had vanished.

"You were great," Liam said to me. "I think that was your best performance."

His compliment did nothing to erase my crankiness over Tessa. Nevertheless, I smiled at my brother. "Thank you."

Chase complimented me too as well as Miller and Woods.

"Here she goes," someone said from the deck above.

I guess she wasn't going to survey the ice farther out.

Tessa shook her wrists a couple of times and began her routine.

Déjà vu hit me. I'd watched Tessa many times, and each time, I bit my nails, my lip, and wrung my hands together, waiting for her to mess up a jump or a spin or anything. But each time, her performance had been spectacular.

Yet this time, she was tense. She skated in a circle—a small circle. The lake was getting to her. As much as I wanted to win, I also wanted to win against a good competitor.

I left Maiken once again and walked out onto the ice when Tessa skated out into a wider arc. Then she went in for her first jump—a Salchow followed by a spin then another.

The guys behind me chatted.

"She's been trying to perfect the triple axel," Chase said. "I think she might try it today."

I hadn't skated long enough to add that difficult jump to my routine. A triple axel required three and half rotations before landing.

Tessa faded from my view. The people on the deck could see her, but I couldn't.

"Where did she go?" Maiken asked.

I skated up to the edge of the deck on the boathouse when someone on the deck above me screamed, "She fell in!"

I blinked several times, rushing farther out onto the ice.

Tessa's arms flailed as she screamed.

I skated as fast as I could to get to her.

"Quinn," Liam shouted. "No. You'll fall in too."

Maybe, but I had to help Tessa no matter how much dissension lay between us.

"I'm slipping," Tessa wailed. "Help me."

I came to an abrupt stop with the edge of my blades, examining the situation.

She braced her elbows on the ice in front of me, which didn't seem weak. I didn't have time to scratch my head as to why the ice had broken.

She sneered up at me. "This is all your fault."

Really? The girl was losing her grip fast, and she had the audacity to blame me. "Shut up, Tessa, and give me your hand." I wasn't strong enough to pull her out, but I had to try.

I checked behind me and found Chase running as best he could on the ice toward us. I wanted to tell him to go back. If we put too much weight on the immediate area around Tessa, we could all go under.

She clutched my gloved hand but slipped away, taking my glove with her.

Damn it.

I tried again. "Come on."

She reached out to me, crying, "Please get me out of here."

Chase finally slid to a stop. "Christ." He held out his hand. "How did this happen?"

We would figure that out later.

Tessa clutched her brother's hand, but his efforts died when his foot slipped out from under him and he fell on his butt.

Then Maiken and Liam came to the rescue.

"Oh shit," Maiken said.

Shit was right. We had to act fast.

I sat down and extended my legs. "I have an idea. Tessa, grab on to my blades. Liam and Chase, try to lift Tessa up by her shoulders. Maiken, I need you to pull me backward. Whatever you do, Tessa, don't let go of my blades." I didn't know if it would work, but we had to try.

Maiken grasped me so that his arms and hands were underneath my armpits. Tessa took hold of my blades with the help of Chase and Liam. Then they grabbed her arms.

"We have to be in sync," Liam said. "Or else this won't work." My brother was in his element, taking charge like he normally did when one of our farm animals needed help. "We do this on three. Maiken, give it all you got, bro. You ready, Chase?"

When Liam shouted "three," we moved, but not by much.

My teeth chattered, as did Tessa's.

"Again," Liam said.

"I don't care if you pull my arms out of the sockets, just get her out of the water," I said.

"Now," Liam shouted.

Maiken yanked me as hard as he could. If my arms were coming out of their sockets, I couldn't tell. In fact, the only thing I could register was my teeth knocking together.

All of a sudden, I was moving, and so was Tessa. We were like hockey pucks as we slid along the ice.

A few feet before we reached the shore, Chase and Liam helped Tessa to stand, but she became a rag doll.

"I got you," Liam said, lifting Tessa into his arms.

She buried her head into the crook of his neck and sobbed.

"Get her up to the house," Kade ordered in a tone that would scare a bear. "Maiken, help Quinn as well. Lacey is filling the bathroom with steam and warm towels."

Maiken came around me, his blue eyes filled with panic. "Give me your hands."

I would have if the blood was flowing through my arms. I inhaled deeply.

Celia rushed up. "Quinn, I don't know whether to be mad at you or not. You could've fallen in too."

I knew that. But someone had needed to help Tessa, and I'd been the best option since I could get to her faster on skates.

Celia and Maiken helped me stand. When I took a step, my knees buckled.

Maiken caught me. "I got you, babe." He wrapped one arm around my waist and the other around my legs. "I'm taking her into the boathouse," he said to Kade.

Kade nodded.

I didn't need special attention like Tessa. Sure, I was cold, but I wasn't soaking wet.

Celia and Maiken guided me up the stairs to the boathouse.

When I reached the top, a redheaded girl who I'd seen in the halls at school said, "You saved Tessa." Her tone was laden with shock and awe.

I suspected her surprise was due to the fact that Tessa and I were enemies. After all, the redhead was there to judge the competition, which had gone viral at school. After what had just happened, I didn't see how people could vote, and that was fine in my book. I didn't need their validation to know that I had skated my best performance. But a deal was a deal, and I wasn't sure what the outcome would be between Tessa and me. At the moment, it didn't matter. Tessa was safe.

Once I was inside and seated on the couch, Maiken turned up the heat while Celia darted back out.

"Are we still voting?" a boy asked outside the window.

I glanced behind me to find Celia shaking her head. "Thank you for coming. We'll be in touch."

"Quinn should win," the boy said. "She rescued Tessa."

I appreciated his comments, although my efforts to save Tessa weren't a reason to win.

The kids on the deck scattered, their footsteps clamoring as they left.

Maiken leaned against the pool table, his expression pensive. "Where did you come up with the idea for Tessa to grab your blades?"

"I don't know. I knew we needed something to anchor her so we could get her out. I can't believe the ice cracked."

"Well, no more skating on it now," Maiken said.

I was cool with that. Besides, I had more important things to do, like resume the conversation we'd started earlier in the bathroom. But before I had the chance, the basketball team converged on the boathouse and I lost Maiken's attention.

Chapter 23

Maiken

The family room was dark, cozy, and warm—a welcome relief to the day before when my body felt like someone had locked me in a freezer for hours on end.

I twirled a strand of Quinn's hair around my finger as we watched the movie *Divergent*. I wasn't really watching, though. I was sifting through the events of the previous day, which had been scary as hell. As much as Tessa wasn't on my list of nice people, no one deserved to fall through the ice. Then when Quinn had taken off after her, my pulse had all but died. Before I'd realized it, I was running out onto the lake like a madman.

Quinn snuggled her head against my chest. "Why are you tense?"

Oh, let's see. You could've died yesterday. Yeah, I'd thought about that all night to the point where sleep had escaped me. Sure, I knew I was being dramatic. But people close to me seemed to be dying, or bad things were happening to them.

Not only that, Kade and I had walked around the lake after everyone had gone home, and we'd found a small stream of water on the east side, flowing into the lake. The warmer water from the stream was probably the culprit that was causing the ice to slowly melt. Thankfully, Quinn hadn't ventured out to the part where Tessa had fallen in.

I kissed her head. "I was thinking about yesterday."

She traced circles on my abs. "It's over with. I'm fine, and so is Tessa."

"Have you talked to her?"

"No," she said. "When I came up to the house to check on her, she was gone. I did see her mom at church this morning, and she said Tessa was fine."

"What about the deal you two made?"

"Do we have to talk about her?"

The subject of Tessa was kind of ruining the mood because now Quinn seemed tense too.

"Let's just watch the movie," I said.

Quinn's finger continued circling around and around on my abs. "You know, I've seen this movie about four times. Maybe we could do something else." She sat up.

I had a feeling I knew what she wanted to do, but I asked just the same. "What do you have in mind?"

Her gaze dropped to my lips.

I grinned, sizing her up. Man, she was so pretty. Her butterscotch hair flowed down around her, framing her delicate face. Her heart-shaped lips were so kissable, and if that didn't ignite all my senses, then the way she looked at me as though no one else existed sure did. I seriously could've stared at her forever.

She pressed her hands to my chest as she straddled me. "No one is home, right?"

Marcus, Jasper, and Ethan were down in the boathouse. Kade was out in the garage, tinkering with an old car the last I knew, and Lacey had taken Emma and the younger kids to the movies.

My grin got bigger, but then the stairs creaked.

Shit. So much for being alone.

"Maiken." Tessa's voice filled the room. "Kade said you were down here."

Quinn flew off me and sat on the cushion beside me as though her father had caught her. Granted, it probably wasn't good for Tessa to see us making out. She might spread a rumor that Quinn and I were naked or something.

Tessa ambled over with her hands tucked into her coat. Her dark gaze regarded me then Quinn. "Just the person I was looking for." Her tone was nice. In fact, she sounded so nice, I could feel my eyebrows rising.

She dropped down in a recliner that was adjacent to the sectional Quinn and I were on. "Oh, I love this movie. *Divergent,* right?"

I snatched the remote and paused the movie.

Silence ticked for a beat as Quinn stared at Tessa with a vacant expression.

Tessa cleared her throat. "I wanted to talk to you about our deal."

Quinn angled her head one way then another, like a puppy trying to figure out what a human was saying.

If Tessa brought up another skating competition, I was nixing the idea. No way was anyone skating on the lake.

Tessa licked her lips. "I want to be head cheerleader next year and the following year. So I would like to clear the air."

Quinn rubbed her hands down her thighs, narrowing her eyes at Tessa. "I'm listening."

I couldn't wait to hear what Tessa had to say. Hopefully, whatever came out of her mouth next would snap the tension between her and Quinn.

Tessa clasped her hands in her lap. "Saying I'm sorry for all the rumors I've spread or stupid things I've said to you isn't going to erase what has already been done. I guess what I'm trying to say is that you're a good person, Quinn. You have a big heart, and if it weren't for you, I wouldn't be sitting here. I see now how much of a bitch I've been to you all these years. We'll never be best friends or even friends, but my bullying days are over."

Quinn's mouth parted in surprise.

Mine did too. Whether Tessa meant what she had just said or not, I believed her. She'd put some heart behind her words.

Tessa rose. "That's all I came to say." She started for the stairs.

Quinn hopped up. "Wait." She strode over to Tessa and threw her arms around her enemy. "I'm glad you're okay."

It took a second for Tessa to return the hug, but she did.

I needed to take a picture to remember this day just in case Tessa decided to renege. But when I reached for my phone from the coffee table, it was too late.

Quinn edged back. "I really would like to see you do a triple axel."

Tessa's eyes widened. "I have a competition coming up next month at the rink if you want to come. It's the week of our February break."

"I would like that," Quinn added.

"You were good out there yesterday," Tessa said. "You should think of competing again."

Quinn shook her head. "Nope. The only time I'll skate is for fun. Don't get me wrong. I love skating, but I would rather do other things." She looked at me.

Tessa laughed. "Boys are definitely fun too."

I hoped I wasn't the reason for Quinn not skating. The last thing I wanted to do was take away a dream of hers. But as I recalled, Quinn had told me her schoolwork was more important since she wanted to be a doctor.

"I need to go," Tessa said. "My mom is waiting for me in the car."

Once Tessa left, Quinn stood motionless.

"Babe, are you okay?"

She pivoted on her heel. "Can you believe what just happened? I've longed for the day when she would leave me alone. Who knew it would take her falling through the ice?"

"It wasn't her falling in, but rather you rescuing her."

Quinn straddled me once again, beaming from ear to ear. "Maybe the next two years will be great." Then her smile faded. "Unless you're moving to Georgia."

Holy crap! I'd forgotten all about that. My mom hadn't made a decision yet. She was taking one day at a time with her sister.

I interlaced my fingers with hers. "Not sure yet. Let's not talk about that."

"Maiken." An edge resonated in her tone. "Can I tell you something?"

My gut twisted, and I wasn't sure if it was in a good way or bad.

"You can tell me anything." *Except if you hate my poem, don't tell me.* She and I hadn't had a chance to pick up where we'd left off the day before when I'd recited the poem to her.

Her chest lifted. "I…" She worried her bottom lip. "I love you." She held her breath.

Whoa! Suddenly, my mouth was as dry as a bone. She certainly held my heart in the palm of her hand. *So, asshat, tell her how you feel.* I would if my tongue would move.

Her face was turning pale as though she regretted saying those three little words.

"Do you remember my poem?" I asked. "I mean, the part where I said you have me under your spell?"

She gnawed hard on her bottom lip as her head moved up and down.

"Well, you do. When I'm not with you, I think about you constantly. And when we're together, all I want to do is kiss you.

You're all beauty and grace, funny and smart, and you make me feel things I've never felt before."

Color returned to her face as a huge smile broke free. "I love your poem by the way."

I kissed her hand. "And I love you too."

I hardly took my next breath before her mouth was on mine. Electricity sparked through me, and I returned the kiss with all I had.

No matter what happened from that moment on, I would always love Quinn Thompson.

Chapter 24

Quinn

A month had passed since that cold day of my skating competition with Tessa. But instead of the ice and snow, I was absorbing the hot sunshine of Georgia during our February break.

I angled my face toward the sky every now and then as I walked along the surf, the waves breaking over my toes.

The last time I'd been to a beach was when I was six. My grandparents had taken Carter, Liam, and me to Cape Code for a long weekend. The only thing I could remember was Granny not letting me near the water without her.

But Granny wasn't with me as I held Maiken's hand. This was one memory I would never forget, and I definitely wouldn't forget the day I'd told him I loved him. That was a day that would be brightly etched in my mind forever. I'd been so darn nervous. But after Tessa and I had had a breakthrough in our relationship, I'd been on cloud nine, wanting to shout to the world not only that Tessa had apologized, but that I loved Maiken Maxwell.

"I'm glad your mom and dad let you come," Maiken said.

When he'd asked me if I wanted to spend our February break in Georgia with him, I'd hurried home from school to ask Momma. I knew it would take some convincing for her and Daddy to say yes. After all, I'd never been away from my parents, and I knew Daddy wouldn't want me to go away with my boyfriend.

"Sweet girl," he said. "You're sixteen, and dashing off with your boyfriend at that age isn't appropriate."

"You don't have to worry about me," I responded. "Kade and Lacey will be there."

Even though Eleanor and Martin had returned from their month-long vacation at the beginning of February, Kade and Lacey were still heavily involved in helping out. Plus, Lacey had to be in Florida for some meetings with the baseball team she played for, and she and Kade had seen an opportunity. They would take the kids down to Georgia, and Lacey would spend a couple of days with Kade before heading to Florida. Then Kade would drive Maiken and his family back to Massachusetts.

"It's not about adults being there," Daddy said. "You're a young woman. He's a young man if you catch my drift."

I kind of suspected that was what he'd been thinking. My mom interjected on my behalf. *Thank God.* I didn't have the courage to talk to my dad about sex without turning a million shades of red.

Anyway, after a heated discussion between my mom and dad, she had given me the thumbs-up.

"I wasn't sure my dad was going to say yes," I said. "After all, I'm his little girl." I didn't want to or wasn't ready to share with Maiken what my dad had been thinking. While I would burn up talking about sex with my dad, I would probably instantly disintegrate if I broached the subject with Maiken.

Our make-out sessions had been limited to kissing only. Neither of us had ventured into groping territory. He was being a gentleman, and if I were being honest, I wasn't ready for more than kissing. Besides, when we were out at Shakers or the movies, we were always surrounded by friends. When I was over at his house, his siblings seemed to barge into the boathouse unexpectedly. If we were in my barn, I was always hyperaware that Carter, Liam, or even Daddy could show up.

Maiken grasped my hand. "My dad wouldn't have allowed Emma to take off for a week with her boyfriend. But I'm glad your dad did say yes."

The beach was deserted except for a jogger or two passing by. I'd learned that morning that the stretch of sand behind Maiken's aunt's home was private.

Speaking of his aunt, she was doing better according to Maiken's mom. The chemo seemed to be working, but her medical team had said she wasn't out of the woods yet. I hadn't had a chance to meet her yet. When we'd arrived the night before, Maiken's mom had informed us that her sister was in the hospital for observation while the medical team ran more tests.

Emma jogged toward us, frayed shorts revealing long legs that glistened in the sunlight. "There you two are. Mom wants to talk to you." Then she ran back to Harlan, Charlotte, and Maple, who were building sandcastles.

"Maybe my mom has good news. Come on." Maiken tugged me along as he picked up the pace.

I was hoping that by good news, he meant he wouldn't be moving next year.

When we trampled up the small path and onto the back deck, Kade was on his phone, and Maiken's mom, Christine, was just coming out of the house. Her eyes were puffy, her skin was ashen, and her brown hair needed a wash.

She squinted, checking on her kids in the distance. Ethan, Marcus, and Jasper were throwing a football well beyond where Emma and the others were.

Maiken left my side to hug his mom. "I hate that you're going through this. You should get some rest while we're here."

She kissed Maiken then let go. "You sound so much like your dad. I'm fine, though. I want to spend time with you. Let's sit."

Kade pocketed his phone and joined us at the glass-topped round table with an overhead umbrella. Then he nodded at Christine for some reason.

"What's going on?" Maiken asked. "Is it Aunt Denise? Did she take a turn for the worse?"

Christine reached over and grasped her son's hand. "She's okay. I wanted to talk to you before I told the others." She sat back in the plastic chair. "I'm so proud of you, Maiken. You've worked hard to improve your grades. I've spoken to your teachers, and they tell me you're doing well in all your subjects. I even spoke to Coach Dean last week, and he tells me the captain position suits you. I knew you were a leader like your dad." She glanced out in the distance.

The lull of the ocean buzzed around us as my pulse hummed along with it. I had a heavy feeling in my stomach that she was trying to find the words to break bad news to Maiken.

Her chest rose and fell. "I'm sorry that your team didn't make the playoffs."

Maiken swung his gaze around the table. "Maybe next year."

Maiken had been bummed that the team had lost more games than they'd won, but Coach Dean had said the guys had come a long way since the beginning of the season.

Hopefully, Maiken would have another chance to lead the team next year.

Christine set her tired gaze on me. "And Quinn, thank you. You've been a great friend to Maiken and our family. Emma talks about you all the time, as does Maiken. So do the others. Harlan can't stop talking about the chickens on your farm."

I blushed. I would do anything for Maiken and his family, and having the kids over to the farm to help feed the chickens, and even the horses and pigs, was nothing. I loved to see Harlan, Charlotte, and Maple's eyes light up when they petted Apple, and I loved how they giggled when the pigs made their signature noises.

"Mom," Maiken said. "You sound like you're going somewhere without us. You're not sick too?" Horror etched his tone.

"Oh, God, no. I'm sorry. This conversation is supposed to be light."

Kade had been quiet, listening and watching. I hadn't known him that well, but in the last month and a half, I'd noticed that he was the silent type, only saying things when he had to. For example, on the way to Georgia, he'd hardly spoken unless it was to talk to Lacey about baseball or reprimand us for getting out of hand in the car.

"I've come to a decision about our living situation," Christine said. "It's not one that I like, but for now, it's best, considering Aunt Denise. But I wanted to get your input before I told your brothers and sisters." She fidgeted in her chair. "I've always, always wanted to keep us all together, but with Aunt Denise, it's going to be difficult unless we find a big home down here, which is impossible financially right now."

Her sister's house only had three bedrooms. It was too tiny for eight kids. In fact, Kade, Lacey, and I were staying at an inn in town while Maiken and his siblings stayed with their mom.

"I also don't want to burden Kade and Lacey or Eleanor and Martin." She looked at Kade. "But Kade and I have talked extensively about this. What do you think about staying with Kade and Lacey for at least your junior year?"

My arm was ready to go up, much like I would do in class when a teacher asked a question. *Pick me. Pick me.*

Kade leaned forward, resting his elbows on the table. His copper eyes shimmered in the sunlight. "Lacey and I have talked. Our new house will be ready by the beginning of summer. So we'll have plenty of room. We would like for you, Emma, and Ethan to live with us, at least until your mom is ready to find a permanent place to settle down."

"I want you kids to stay in one place, especially through high school," Christine said. "This is the time to make long-term friends, focus on your studies so colleges will look at you. Sure, you can do the same here in Georgia, but you seem to like Kensington."

I had one leg crossed over the other, moving my foot furiously.

Maiken looked at me as though he wanted to know what I thought. All I did was smile. The selfish part of me wanted to nudge him along. I wanted him to stay at Kensington for the next two years. The unselfish side of me wanted to encourage him to stay with his family. After all, family was important to him, and I couldn't fault him for that. If I were in his shoes, I would struggle with my decision.

But Kensington was a great school. He was captain of the basketball team. He wouldn't have to make new friends, and he had me.

"So Emma and Ethan don't know yet?" Maiken asked.

"No," Christine said. "I'm asking you first because they'll make their decision based on what you decide."

Maiken looked out at his brothers and sisters. "What about Marcus? He'll be starting high school. He'll be alone down here with Jasper in junior high."

"He has a point, Christine," Kade said. "We'll have plenty of bedrooms in our new house."

"Let's table that for now. We'll talk more when school ends." Christine looked out at her kids. "Maiken, I want you to be happy. I don't want you to worry about your brothers and sisters. Enjoy your high school years."

Maiken adjusted himself in his chair. "So all of us will stay in Ashford until the summer?"

"Right now, that's the plan," she said. "If Aunt Denise continues to improve, then I'll consider finding a home in Ashford."

"You hate the weather," Maiken said.

"Sure, but I love my kids, and there's nothing better to a mother than seeing her children happy. Besides, we have more family in Ashford than here in Georgia."

Maiken grabbed my hand. "What do you think?"

My eyes went wide, and my heart was beating all over the place. He knew I didn't want him to leave. He knew I would probably die if he did.

Kade and Christine waited patiently for my answer. Maiken, however, rubbed his thumb on the back of my hand.

"It's a tough decision," I finally said. "But you have to decide what will make you happy."

Kade tapped his heart. "What's in here?"

Maiken grinned like he was remembering something. "The heart knows." He sighed. "Mom, I would like to finish high school at Kensington on one condition."

One of her eyebrows quirked up.

"If you need me, you'll tell me," Maiken said. "I'll move in a heartbeat."

Christine broke out with a warm, motherly smile. "I wouldn't hesitate. I love you, Maiken. You're so much like your father."

I wished I'd gotten to meet his father, but right now I wanted nothing more than to throw myself at Maiken. But Christine beat me to it.

Instead, I sighed heavily. Kade chuckled as though he knew the tension I'd been under.

Christine then traded Maiken for me. "You're a good girl, Quinn. I'm so glad Maiken loves you."

Happy tears surfaced. As much as I appreciated her words and gesture, I wanted to feel Maiken's arms around me.

Christine must've sensed my impatience because she said, "Kade, why don't we head down to the beach and see the kids?"

When Maiken and I were alone on the deck, he hung his head. I couldn't tell how he was feeling.

I linked my fingers with his. "Talk to me."

A light breeze ruffled his hair, making him more handsome, if that were possible. "I feel like a weight was just lifted off my shoulders."

No doubt.

Then he flattened his hands against my cheeks. "Are you sure you want me around next year?" he teased.

I rolled my eyes. "Mmm."

Whatever else I was about to say or had on my mind blew away with the ocean breeze when his lips grazed mine. "It's you and me, Quinn Thompson. Let's make great high school memories together."

Eeek. I was all for that. With Maiken at my side, our high school years were going to be epic.

Epilogue

Maiken

The school year had ended the week before, and excitement charged the air. My siblings and I were waiting for Uncle Martin. He'd gone to pick up the boat that had been in the shop for the last two weeks. He was also having the new name of Harlan Marlin imprinted on the back. He'd loved Ethan's idea of dedicating the boat to his brother.

Harlan squealed as he splashed water at Charlotte, who in turn screamed at him from the water's edge.

I stood ankle deep, watching Harlan and Charlotte have a great time swimming around.

The trees rustled around the lake as the sun glinted off the water. No more snow. No more freezing temperatures, and no more ice.

"Quinn!" Harlan shouted.

I turned to find my girl sashaying down from the garage, dressed in jean shorts and a tank top, with her hair pulled up in a high ponytail.

The temperatures for June had been in the low eighties with an off-the-charts humidity level—a huge change from the freezing temperatures that past winter.

Quinn was holding something in her hand as she waved. Her

face broke out in an award-winning smile that always made my body sing.

Then it dawned on me. She'd gone to get her driver's license.

"I got it," she squealed.

I stepped out of the water, lifted her up, and swung her around. "I'm so proud of you."

She giggled as I set her down. "I was nervous. So nervous."

Harlan ran out of the water and threw himself at Quinn. She barely had time to catch him as his soaking-wet body plastered against her. "What did you get?"

She squatted down and showed Harlan her license. "I can drive a car now. See?"

He looked at her picture. "You're pretty."

She ruffled his wet hair. "And you're handsome."

"I know," he said matter-of-factly.

I couldn't help but laugh.

"Maiken," Kade called from the garage. "My dad is coming down the road."

"Oooh," Quinn said. "The boat."

Charlotte ran out of the water and kept running up the grassy hill to the garage. Harlan was right behind her.

"Do you want to go swimming later?" I asked.

Quinn glanced out at the water, her amber eyes shimmering. "Can you believe that not five months ago, I was ice-skating on the lake?"

And fighting with Tessa Stevens, who had since backed off on bullying Quinn. They weren't friends by any means, but it had been nice not to hear Tessa throw out taunts at Quinn or snarl at her every chance she had in the halls at school. Whether the nicer side of Tessa Stevens would continue in our junior year was yet to be seen, but that was something to worry about next year. With the summer upon us, I doubted Quinn or I would see Tessa Stevens.

I chuckled. "I can't believe I stood out in the middle when the lake was one solid piece of ice."

"When are you leaving for Georgia?" she asked.

I dried my feet on a towel. "Next week."

The plan was to spend a month in Georgia with Mom and Aunt Denise, who was holding her own considering all the chemo she'd had, then return the month before school started to get settled into Kade and Lacey's new home.

"I'll miss you." Quinn sounded sad all of a sudden.

I tugged her to me and wrapped my arms around her. "We'll talk every day and text all the time. Besides, you're still coming for a few days in July. Right?"

She eased back. "Of course. After my visit to North Carolina State."

Quinn, Liam, and their mom were visiting colleges that Liam and Quinn were interested in. I knew I needed to start thinking more seriously about colleges, but life had been so busy. I wished the basketball team had had a better season. We hadn't made the play-offs, but we'd had a couple of scouts at our home games. I was pretty sure they'd come to see Liam.

According to Coach Dean, scouts looked at everyone, but they didn't get serious about offers usually until junior and senior years, and Liam would be a senior next year. I was happy for him. He was interested in Georgetown, which was one of the Thompsons' stops on the way to NC State. But NC State was interested in him over Georgetown. Not only that, NC State was one of Quinn's college choices. Apparently, they had a great premed program.

"See? Then we'll only be apart for three weeks."

She giggled. "Things are looking up."

The sound of an engine grew louder, announcing the arrival of Uncle Martin.

I grasped Quinn's hand. "Come on. I don't want to miss this."

We jogged up to the garage just as Uncle Martin's truck came down the driveway.

Kade, Aunt Eleanor, and all my brothers and sisters stood on the deck, tittering and giggling.

Uncle Martin turned and parked in front of the six-bay garage so that the truck and boat were parallel to it, with the back of the boat facing us. We couldn't see the name yet since a red cover masked the boat.

Uncle Martin climbed out, grinning at everyone. He reminded me of an older version of Kade.

The kids ran down off the deck. Quinn and I ambled closer to the boat, and Aunt Eleanor and Kade joined us.

"Are you ready to see?" Uncle Martin asked, standing at the back edge of the boat.

Everyone squealed in delight.

"Maiken," Uncle Martin said. "You have some words you want to say?"

Kade took up a position opposite his dad. Both were ready to unveil the name.

I left Quinn near Aunt Eleanor, Ethan, and Emma, who all stood behind Marcus, Jasper, Maple, Charlotte, and Harlan.

My heart rate sped up as I stood in front of the boat and faced my siblings. I thought it would be easy to talk about my dad, but as I looked at my brothers and sisters, I wasn't sure I could say anything without crying.

"Hurry up, Maiken," Emma said, prodding me with her eyes.

I cleared the emotion from my throat, stood up a little straighter, and smiled. "Kade and Lacey told us to find something to celebrate Dad. And Ethan is a genius for coming up with the idea of naming the boat after him." I nodded to my brother, who seemed proud. "But it's not just the boat that we need to remember Dad by." I touched my heart. "He's in here. And wherever we go or wherever we live, we need to keep Dad close to our hearts."

Jasper's blond hair ruffled in the warm breeze. "I'm going to build a model boat this summer. We'll name that one Harlan Marlin too."

The boat wasn't like the memorial that Kade and his brothers had built for Karen on the other side of the lake, where we could visit anytime. Nevertheless, I loved that Jasper was thinking of his own way to remember Dad.

"Show us already," Marcus said.

I stepped out of the way and off to the side.

Kade and Uncle Martin removed the cover.

An intake of breath zipped around the group along with oohs and aahs.

Harlan went up to the boat and touched Dad's name. "That's my name too."

Everyone laughed.

The name was scripted in royal blue with the H in Harlan and the M in Marlin larger than the rest of the letters.

Each of us mimicked Harlan by touching Dad's name as tears flowed from mostly everyone.

I was the last to touch his name, and when I did, a warm feeling spread through my chest. It was as though my dad was speaking to me in some way. I knew that sounded crazy. I just felt like he was with us, and for that, I wiped away my tears and smiled.

"I'm going to put the boat in the water," Uncle Martin said. "Head down to the lake."

My younger siblings took off, and the older ones lingered behind.

"Do you want to go with us?" I asked Quinn.

She pointed up toward the front of the house. "I need to get home. Liam's waiting for his truck."

"What about swimming?" I'd asked her that earlier, but she'd never responded.

She kissed me on the lips. "Spend time with your family. We can swim tomorrow."

I did want to enjoy the time with my brothers and sisters while we were all still together. Next year, Jasper, Maple, Harlan, and Charlotte were going to school in Georgia, while Ethan, Emma, and I were returning to Kensington. And Marcus would be joining us now that he was going to be a freshman in high school.

Kade and Mom had talked, and both felt it was best if Marcus was in school with Ethan, Emma, and me. Otherwise, he would be attending high school all by himself in Georgia since Jasper would still be in middle school.

I walked Quinn up to Liam's truck. "Thank you."

She furrowed her eyebrows. "For what?"

"For being a great girlfriend. I mean, I don't want you to go, but I do want to hang out with my family."

She poked me in the arm. "I love you, Maiken Maxwell. Family is important. Besides, we have all next year and even most of the summer. I'm just sad we won't see each other for a few weeks."

I loved this girl so hard, and whatever was in store for us in the near future, I was glad she was at my side.

DEAR READER

I hope you enjoyed reading about all the new Maxwells, and the continuation of Maiken and Quinn's story. There will be two more books to finish Maiken and Quinn's story. Come join us in Maxwell Mania and stay up-to-date on Maxwell news: Facebook: https://www.facebook.com/groups/maxwellmania/

When you have a moment, I would super appreciate a quick review. It doesn't have to be long, but would love for you to share your excitement about My Heart to Hold. You can leave a review on Amazon, Goodreads or Bookbub . Links to these platforms can be found on the next page.

Reading Order for the Maxwell Family Saga Series.

- Book 1: My Heart to Touch
- Book 2: May Heart to Hold
- Book 3: My Heart to Give - *Coming Soon*
- Book 4: My Heart to Keep - *Coming Soon*

Have you read Kade Maxwell's story? If not, check out the first book in the Maxwell Series (Dare to Kiss) and meet Kade, Kelton, Kross, and Kody. http://sbalexander.com/book-series/the-maxwell-series/page/2/

DON'T MISS OUT

Stay up-to-date on sales and new releases. I post frequent updates in my reader group on Facebook. You can join here: Maxwell Mania: https://www.facebook.com/groups/maxwellmania/
Follow me on any of the platforms below or signup for my newsletter at http://sbalexander.com/newsletter or visit my website at http://sbalexander.com

ALSO BY S.B. ALEXANDER

To read samples and find out where to purchase all books visit:
http://sbalexander.com.

The Maxwell Family Saga:

My Heart to Touch - Book 1

My Heart to Hold – Book 2

My Heart to Give – Book 3 (releasing 2019)

My Heart to Keep - Book 4 (releasing 2019)

The Maxwell Series:

Dare to Kiss - Book 1

Dare to Dream – Book 2

Dare to Love – Book 3

Dare to Dance - Book 4

Dare to Live - Book 5

Dare to Breathe - Book 6

The Maxwell Series Boxed Set – Books 1-3

The Maxwell Series Boxed Set - Books 4-6

Dare to Kiss Coloring Book Companion

The Vampire SEAL Series:

On the Edge of Humanity – Book 1

On the Edge of Eternity – Book 2

On the Edge of Destiny – Book 3

On the Edge of Misery - Book 4

On the Edge of Infinity - Book 5

The Vampire SEAL Collection - Boxed Set

Stand Alone Books

Breaking Rules

Rescuing Riley

The Hart Series:

Hart of Darkness

Hart of Vengeance - Coming Soon

Hart of Redemption - Coming Soon

ACKNOWLEDGMENTS

Writing and publishing a book takes a village. But I couldn't be more thankful to the one person who gives me the inspiration to do what I love—my husband. He's been such a guiding light as he battles one of the worse diseases with no cure. He fills my heart with so much joy. He always has a smile on his face, he's always laughing, and he's always making sure I'm taken care of. He's my angel. I couldn't do this without him.

I'm also grateful to the team behind me who helps me every step of the way from my editor, RedAdept Editing, my beta readers, my ARC team, my cover designer, Hang Le, and everyone in Maxwell Mania. Thank you, thank you, thank you!

A big hug and mad love for Heather Carver for keeping me focused and motivating me everyday to write, and to Kylie Sharp for always being a phone call away. Love you gals.

Finally, to all the readers and bloggers around the world, thank you for taking a chance on me.

www.ingramcontent.com/pod-product-compliance
Lightning Source LLC
Chambersburg PA
CBHW071118100726
47908CB00008B/2418

9 781732 976733